The Map Trap

Also by Andrew Clements

A Million Dots
About Average

Benjamin Pratt & the Keepers of the School
We the Children
Fear Itself
The Whites of Their Eyes
In Harm's Way
We Hold These Truths

Big Al
Big Al and Shrimpy
Dogku
Extra Credit
Frindle
The Handiest Things in the World
Jake Drake, Bully Buster
Jake Drake, Class Clown
Jake Drake, Know-It-All
Jake Drake, Teacher's Pet
The Jacket
The Janitor's Boy
The Landry News
The Last Holiday Concert
Lost and Found
Lunch Money
No Talking
The Report Card
Room One
The School Story
Troublemaker
A Week in the Woods

The Map Trap

Andrew Clements

Illustrations by Dan Andreasen

Atheneum Books for Young Readers
New York · London · Toronto · Sydney · New Delhi

atheneum

ATHENEUM BOOKS FOR YOUNG READERS

An imprint of Simon & Schuster Children's Publishing Division

1230 Avenue of the Americas, New York, New York 10020

ATHENEUM BOOKS FOR YOUNG READERS is a registered trademark of Simon & Schuster, Inc.

Atheneum logo is a trademark of Simon & Schuster, Inc.

For information about special discounts for bulk purchases, please contact Simon & Schuster Special Sales at 1-866-506-1949 or business@simonandschuster.com.

The Simon & Schuster Speakers Bureau can bring authors to your live event. For more information or to book an event, contact the Simon & Schuster Speakers Bureau at 1-866-248-3049 or visit our website at www.simonspeakers.com.

Also available in an Atheneum Books for Young Readers hardcover edition.

Interior design by Mike Rosamilia, cover design by Lauren Rille

The text for this book is set in Bembo.

The illustrations for this book are rendered in pencil.

Manufactured in the United States of America

0621 OFF

First Atheneum Books for Young Readers paperback edition July 2016

10 9 8 7 6

The Library of Congress has cataloged the hardcover edition as follows:

Library of Congress Cataloging-in-Publication Data

Clements, Andrew, 1949-

The map trap / Andrew Clements ; illustrated by Dan Andreasen. — First edition.

pages cm

Summary: Sixth-grader Alton Ziegler loves maps, and when his folder of secret maps is stolen, he begins getting notes with orders that he must obey to get the maps back but, with the help of a popular classmate, he just might succeed before his teacher, principal, or someone else learns he has been studying and mapping things about them.

ISBN 978-1-4169-9727-6 (hc)

ISBN 978-1-4169-9728-3 (pbk)

ISBN 978-1-4169-9729-0 (eBook)

[1. Maps—Fiction. 2. Cartography—Fiction. 3. Schools—Fiction. 4. Friendship—Fiction. 5. Stealing—Fiction. 6. Mystery and detective stories.] I. Title.

PZ7.C59118Map 2014

[Fic]—dc23   2014006821

For Joan Franklin Smutny,
whose care and guidance helped me
become a classroom teacher
—A.C.

Acknowledgments

Thanks to Ken Jennings for the enlightening first-person account in his book *Maphead*. Thanks also to the great cartographers, past and present, at the National Geographic Society, and to the many geniuses who have made GPS navigation available and understandable and practical. The blog "Strange Maps" by Frank Jacobs was a source of frequent inspiration about the unlimited possibilities of maps and mapping. With this book, as with many others, Caitlyn Dlouhy at Atheneum Books for Young Readers helped me find my way from a first draft to the final text, and I am deeply appreciative. Above all, I am grateful for my wife, Rebecca, who keeps me grounded and happy and moving forward.

CHAPTER ONE

BAD HAIR DAY

When the fire alarm began to beep and blink on Tuesday morning, the first thing Miss Wheeling thought about was her hair. She'd been outside on bus duty forty minutes ago, and it was a bright October day, moist and windy—the worst kind of weather for her hair. Couldn't the principal have put off this drill for a couple of days?

It was free-activity time near the end of homeroom, and she clapped her hands sharply. "All right, everyone, this is a fire drill. Line up quickly, and I want you *quiet*! And don't clean up, don't do anything except get in line right *now*!"

She wrestled a scarf around her hair, and then, clutching her clipboard, Miss Wheeling led her homeroom students down the hall, past the gym, and straight outside toward their assigned spot along the playground fence. She noted with pride that hers was one of the first groups out of the building—pretty good for a brand-new teacher! She hoped the principal would notice.

She tried to remember the last time she'd been part of a fire drill, but she couldn't get a clear picture. . . . It had probably been during high school—about five years ago, back when she was just Holly Wheeling, that girl who was crazy about insects.

She heard some loud whispering behind her, but she didn't need to look to know who it was. This class had a handful of very gabby kids.

"Annie and Kelley? I asked you *not* to talk. A fire drill is serious business."

She still felt amazed every time she realized that now she was Miss Wheeling, *the teacher*. She looked young, she felt young—she *was* young, only twenty-three years old. In fact, her own little brother was twelve, the same age as most of her students. And she was *very* glad that her family lived in Cedar Falls, Iowa, instead of Harper's Grove, Illinois—the town where she now lived and worked. The thought of being Carl's teacher? It was enough to give a girl nightmares.

The wind kicked up a flurry of dead leaves along the playground fence, and Miss Wheeling held the corners of her scarf tightly under her chin. But she knew it was hopeless. This was going to be a bad hair day—mega-bad. She'd been trying to set an appointment for a haircut for the past three weeks, but her first months as a new teacher had been insanely busy. Not that haircuts ever helped much. Her hair was very full, extremely curly, and almost impossible to style. She'd been fighting with it almost every day since she was about six years old. And losing.

All the classes were outside now, and she saw Mrs. Buckley at the far side of the playground. The principal was moving from teacher to teacher, checking off each group.

Miss Wheeling whipped her scarf off her head and stuffed it into the back pocket of her slacks. She looked at her clipboard and called out, "Billy Atkinson?"

"Here."

"Jada Bartlett?"

"Present."

"Carson Burr?"

"Present."

Miss Wheeling hurried through the names as the principal came nearer, and finally called out, "Alton Ziegler?"

Nothing.

She called the name again. "Alton Ziegler?"

The principal was close now, talking with Mr. Troy, the other sixth-grade teacher.

Desperate, Miss Wheeling flipped to her attendance sheets . . . but Alton was definitely present today. She was certain that she'd seen him just half an hour ago, and she was sure—

"Good morning, Miss Wheeling." Mrs. Buckley smiled at her and then at the kids. "Is your class all accounted for?"

"I'm . . . I'm sorry, but Alton Ziegler's not here." Miss Wheeling felt her face growing pale, and her hands were cold and clammy. She felt light-headed.

The principal frowned. "Was he in homeroom when you took attendance?"

"Oh . . . oh, yes! I checked him off, see?" Helplessly, Miss Wheeling held out her clipboard.

Mrs. Buckley didn't look at it. With a sharp edge to her voice, she said, "I'll stay with your class. Go and find him. Right now."

Miss Wheeling half walked, half ran to the gym door, and she could feel the eyes of everyone in the school watching her—and watching the way her hair bounced around as she ran.

Breathless now, she sprinted to her classroom door, but it was locked—and she didn't have a key.

As she started to turn to go find the janitor, she spotted something on the far side of the room, over beyond the desks, by the windows. Something on the floor.

It was a shoe, a boy's sneaker.

Leaning forward, she pressed her nose against the glass and cupped her hands around her eyes and forehead to block the glare from the hallway lights.

It was definitely a shoe—and also an ankle, plus six inches of a leg . . . wearing blue jeans!

With one hand she banged on the door, still looking at that foot. She called out, "Alton? Alton . . . ? Is that you? *Alton!* Answer me!"

The shoe, the foot, the leg—nothing moved.

Miss Wheeling yelled down the hallway. "Mr. Sims? *Mr. Sims!* Can you hear me?"

"I'm in the front hall," he called back. "What's up?"

"An emergency in room forty-three! Bring a key, and *hurry*!"

Miss Wheeling heard a sharp *crack* as a wooden broom handle hit the floor, and then jangling keys as the janitor came around the corner at a dead run. A moment later he unlocked her door and shoved it open.

She dashed in, fearing the worst. Rounding the last row of desks along the windows, Miss Wheeling stopped—and stared.

She had a clear view of the whole scene—shoe, ankle, leg . . . the entire boy. Alton Zeigler was propped up on his elbows in a patch of sunlight. White wires from a small iPod ran to his ears, and a large sheet of paper lay before him, with markers and colored pencils spread about. He held a red pen in his right hand, and he was humming a tune she didn't know. Mr. Sims stood beside her.

Miss Wheeling reached out her toe and tapped Alton's foot, and he jumped like he'd been stung by a bee. He spun around, then smiled and pulled out his earbuds. He glanced from Miss Wheeling to the janitor.

"Hi—what are you guys doing here?"

Holly Wheeling had trouble finding words—all her fear had turned to anger. She wanted to shout, *What are* we *doing here? What in the world are* you *doing here?!*

But that would have been pointless, because it was perfectly clear what Alton Zeigler was doing here.

He was making a map.

CHAPTER TWO

THE MAKING OF A MAP NUT

It wasn't like there had been some kind of a master plan to try to turn Alton Zeigler into a map nut. In fact, *lack* of planning is sort of what started it all.

Because if Alton's mom and dad had planned better, they would have studied one of those "name your baby" books, and they would have had a name all picked out a month before their son was born.

But they hadn't done that.

And therefore, as his dad was driving Alton's mom to the hospital, she pulled a coffee-stained Illinois road map from the pocket of the car door, unfolded it, and began reading aloud from the long list of town names.

"... Alma, Alorton, Alpha, Alsey, Alsip, Altamont, Alto Pass, Alton, Altona, Alvan, Amboy—"

"Wait!" his dad said. "That was it!"

His mom made a face. "What—*Amboy*? That's a terrible name for a—"

"No, no," his dad said, "*Alton!* Alton Zeigler!"

"Alton Zeigler," his mom repeated, and then she said it again slowly: "Alton Zeigler." She smiled. "It sounds good, don't you think? *Alton*—I like it!"

"Me too," said his dad. "And his nickname can be Al—it's great!"

"Al?" She turned and stared at him. "No, dear, not Al—never. His name is Alton—period."

Six hours later, Alton Robert Zeigler was the name they wrote on the new birth certificate.

And six days later, his parents had framed that map of Illinois, coffee stains and all, and they put it up on the wall right next to their baby's new crib.

Every time little Alton was put into bed, he lay on his back, looking up, and the map was there. He would fall asleep, and when he woke up, there it was again, day after day after day.

Of course, early on, Alton saw that map only as a big white-and-yellow blob, all crisscrossed with black, red, green, blue, and yellow lines. And he didn't even have names for those colors, not in the beginning. But he looked and he looked, and he noticed everything.

When the rest of the family learned how Alton had gotten his name, mappish things began to happen.

His uncle Robert bought his little nephew an inflatable globe, sort of like a giant beach ball. Except it wasn't for bouncing around. It was a night-light, lit from the inside by a small LED. And Uncle Robert helped Alton's mom and dad hang it from the ceiling in the center of the nursery.

The oceans were blue, the deserts were brown, the mountains were green, and the countries were all the colors of the rainbow. And everywhere, thin black lines ran side to side and top to bottom.

Of course, little Alton didn't understand any of what he saw—not at the beginning. But the globe was there every night, glowing in the dark sky of his room, and he looked and he looked, and he noticed everything.

Grandma Susie out in Arizona heard the story of Alton's name, and she looked online and found a pretty rug for his nursery floor—a rug that was also a map of the United States. It showed the name of each state and its capital city, plus a big blue star for Washington, D.C. And when Alton

first got up onto his hands and knees, his mother called Grandma Susie and said, "Guess what, Mom! Alton just crawled all the way from Texas to Michigan!"

Alton's other grandparents lived in Connecticut, and they played a part in the map nuttiness too, but it wasn't something they did on purpose. They had given a present to Alton's mom and dad the first Christmas after they got married—a subscription to *National Geographic* magazine. And his grandparents kept on renewing the subscription, year after year.

Alton was born five years after that subscription began, so there was already a full shelf of the bright yellow magazines in a bookcase in the family room. By the time Alton turned seven, there were more than a hundred different issues of *National Geographic* at his house.

And one rainy Sunday afternoon, as seven-year-old Alton sat looking at some pictures of a temple in Tibet, he turned a page, and a heavy sheet of folded paper fell to the floor. He opened it and flattened it out, and stared down at a map called "China and the Forbidden City."

The map was big—even bigger than the old road map hanging on the wall in his room. He had never seen a map so colorful and so packed with facts.

He picked it up and ran to show his mom and dad. "Look! This was inside that old *National Geographic*—isn't it great?!"

They helped him spread it out on the kitchen table, then leaned over it with him.

After a minute his mom said, "It's pretty amazing—I love the drawings of the palace, don't you?"

And his dad said, "Yeah, great map—and guess what? If you go look through the other *National Geographics*, I bet you'll find a bunch more."

The hunt was on, and Alton whipped through those magazines like a tornado—first the ones in the family room, then the older copies on the shelves in the basement.

Two hours later he called out, "Hey, come quick! I need help!"

His dad got to Alton's bedroom first.

"What's the—" He stopped. And stared.

Alton's mom finished the question: "Problem?" She was staring too.

Every bit of wall space in Alton's room had been covered with maps. And they weren't just taped up all higgledy-piggledy. Maps about Asia filled half a wall, then to the left of them came maps about Europe. The other continents followed, from east to west and north to south. There was also a sprinkling of maps about the oceans and animals and natural resources, plus a handful that featured major historical events or ancient civilizations. Using about thirty maps, Alton had created a grand tour of the whole Earth.

And now he stood on top of some books stacked on his desk chair. "I have to get these other ones up onto the ceiling."

Ten minutes later Alton and his parents were lying on their backs across his bed, looking up at maps about the moon, Mars, the solar system, and the whole universe, plus a really great map called "The History of Flight." There was also one called "Planet of the Dinosaurs," which didn't really fit in with the other stuff on the ceiling, but it was about dinosaurs, so it *had* to go somewhere.

This was a big event for Alton, a major mapquake, and it shook up his view of the world. It also taught him how maps could be used to show all kinds of different information—and it happened in October of his second-grade year.

By October of his fourth-grade year, Alton's collection of maps had grown to more than a hundred and fifty. Fourth grade was also the year he began to get serious about drawing maps of his own.

He discovered that making a good map was complicated, much more complicated than he had ever imagined. And even though he didn't like math very much, he made himself learn about fractions and measurement so that his maps could be as accurate as possible. He didn't really notice it, but during fourth grade, maps began to turn him into a very precise thinker and a very careful observer.

And by October of his sixth-grade year, Alton Robert Zeigler had become well known at Harper School as a complete geo-geek—the kind of kid who could get so wrapped up in drawing a new map that he wouldn't even notice when his whole class lined up and hurried out of the room for a fire drill.

Because when Miss Wheeling and Mr. Sims found him Tuesday morning, lying on the floor by the windows in room forty-three, that's certainly the way things looked.

But any good mapmaker knows that the way things *look* and the way things *are* can sometimes be different.

Very different.

CHAPTER THREE

LIKE SWITZERLAND

Once most of the classes were back inside after the fire drill, Mr. Sims went into the janitor's workroom. He sat at his desk, then swiveled his chair toward his assistant, who was standing at the workbench.

"Funny thing just happened."

Joe Herrin looked up from the valve he was fixing. "What'd you say?"

"I said, a funny thing just happened."

"Yeah? What?"

"During the fire drill, that new teacher yelled for me—an emergency in her room. So I ran down there."

"Which teacher?"

"The young one, with the big hair."

"Oh, right. And?"

"Her door was locked, so I opened it up. And

you know what the emergency was? That Ziegler kid—he was lying on the floor by the windows drawing a map, headphones stuck in his ears. She had to kick his foot to get his attention, and then he looked all surprised said, 'What are you guys doing here?'"

Joe grinned and nodded. "That *is* funny! I've always liked that kid."

Mr. Sims said, "Yeah, except *that's* not the funny part. It was the way the kid looked at us. Because he *wasn't* surprised to see us, not at all. A little scared, a little jumpy, but not surprised. Maybe that teacher can't spot the tricks yet, but *I* know a fake-out when I see one. And that kid was faking like crazy."

Joe stopped grinning. "So . . . how come?"

The janitor shrugged. "Beats me. But that kid was up to something. No doubt about it."

Joe thought a second. "You gonna tell Miss What's-Her-Name?"

Mr. Sims shook his head. "Nope. I'm neutral . . . just like Switzerland. Until a kid starts breaking windows or throwing snowballs in the gym, I'm neutral." He stood up. "We'd better go sweep up the stuff everybody just tracked inside. Hit the west hallway when you're done with that valve, okay?"

Joe said, "Sure thing . . . Mr. Switzerland."

CHAPTER FOUR

CONSEQUENCES

The final bell had rung, and the school was beginning to get quiet. It was Holly Wheeling's favorite time of day.

"Um, Miss Wheeling?"

She looked up from the papers on her desk, and when she saw who it was, her eyes narrowed and her mouth formed a small frown.

"Hello, Alton."

Alton seemed tongue-tied, but Miss Wheeling didn't help him out. She just waited. He looked right into her face, but then he blinked and dropped his gaze, his dark eyebrows scrunched together, almost touching. She had noticed his eyebrows did that whenever he concentrated on something.

"Um, I . . . I'm sorry," he said, looking at her again. "Sorry that you got in trouble because of me missing the fire drill this morning."

Miss Wheeling almost melted. His brown eyes looked so sad and sweet—a lot like the eyes of her golden retriever, Mr. Wiggles.

But to just smile and say, *Oh, it's all right, Alton—I know you didn't do it on purpose*. . . . No, that would have been letting him off way too easy. After all, it *was* partly his fault . . . wasn't it? And there ought to be consequences for him . . . right?

Because there certainly were some consequences for her.

She'd had a meeting with the principal during her afternoon preparation period, and Mrs. Buckley had asked her to review the school's fire-drill procedures and then write up recommendations to insure that every child was accounted for at every moment.

It wasn't exactly a punishment, but that's how it felt. Losing track of a student during a fire drill was bad. And for a first-year teacher? This incident would certainly get written up and be placed in her personnel folder. It might even be the kind of thing that could keep a brand-new teacher like her from getting a permanent job.

Alton stood there, looking sorrier and sorrier.

She knew that he really was a nice kid—sort of on the quiet side, and definitely too crazy about maps . . . but that wasn't a crime, right? Kids got super-interested in lots of things—dinosaurs, NASCAR, video games, soccer, pop music stars, baseball . . . it was a long list. Not too many years ago, she could remember being completely nuts about everything concerning the wreck of the *Titanic*. She'd watched a dozen movies and documentaries about it, practically memorized the names of everyone who died, and had even tried writing letters to the grandchildren of some of the survivors. And before the *Titanic*, it had been glaciers, and before that, cheetahs, and before that, beetles. So it didn't seem weird that Alton was so hooked on cartography.

Today Alton was wearing a T-shirt with a map of the Illinois State Fairgrounds on the front.

He always wore jeans and a T-shirt, and the shirt always had some kind of map on it. She'd asked him about his shirts once, and he told her that he searched online for most of them, and that his relatives were always sending him new ones too. He really was a cute kid . . . a lot like her little brother—except Carl teased her a lot. And she knew for a fact that Carl's teachers thought he was a major smart aleck. And Alton wasn't like that.

"So, um . . . that's all I wanted to tell you," he said, sort of shrugging a little. "That I was sorry."

Miss Wheeling gave him a smile—she couldn't help herself.

"It's all right, Alton. Go on and catch your bus now. Have a good night, and I'll see you tomorrow. And you'll have to show me the map you were working on today, okay? And I forgive you—I know you didn't miss the fire drill on purpose!"

Alton managed a polite nod, and said, "Thanks. See you tomorrow."

He still looked miserable, and Miss Wheeling was surprised that he didn't brighten up a little or even smile. But sometimes boys were more sensitive than they let on—she remembered that from a child development course she'd taken last year.

Miss Wheeling had read Alton's face correctly: He really did feel miserable as he left her room— even worse than before he had apologized.

But she never could have guessed *why* Alton felt so bad.

Miss Wheeling didn't know that what she had just said to him kept replaying in his mind: *I know you didn't miss the fire drill on purpose!*

Because the truth was, he *had* missed it on purpose. Completely.

And the reason?

Like almost everything else in Alton's life, the reason had something to do with maps.

CHAPTER FIVE

FOLDER

Alton frowned as he looked out the bus window at the blur of cornfields, brown and almost ready to harvest. His house was only 2.214 miles due west of the school parking lot, but the bus stopped seventeen times before it got there. So the ride home was a good time to think.

This whole situation? It's my own stupid fault!

And really, he was right about that.

About a week ago, he had started trying to be friends with Quint Harrison. Quint sat right behind him during social studies, and he always watched Alton draw and doodle during class. Mr. Troy talked a lot, so there was usually plenty of time for drawing.

"Yo, Al—that is so *awesome!*"

That was what Quint would whisper over his shoulder.

Or sometimes he'd say, "*Excellent!* Really, dude, that is *wicked* cool!"

Alton hated slang. And he had to keep reminding Quint that his name *wasn't* Al—it was Alton.

Why did I think I could be friends with a guy who sounds like he escaped from a 1980s TV show?

Why? The truth was hard to admit, but Alton faced it: When Quint had begun to compliment him, he'd felt flattered.

Quint always hung out with the popular kids, and Alton never did. Quint seemed to really like Alton's drawings and diagrams—even when Alton knew they were nowhere near his best work. And somewhere in the back of his mind, he started thinking about what it would be like to have Quint say hi to him in the halls or joke around with him during lunch or maybe even hang out with him after school—and do things like play video games or watch movies . . . or whatever the popular kids did when they weren't being wicked awesome and totally cool at school.

And as Alton kept imagining the good times he could have with his new friend, in another corner of his mind he heard his mom asking him, "Did you make any new friends at school?"

She said that a lot.

Which seemed pretty stupid to Alton, because he already had friends—Christopher, for example.

Chris's parents and his parents vacationed in rented cabins at Lake Mendota in Wisconsin every summer, and he and Chris had been friends ever since they were three years old. Just this last summer they'd gone swimming or fishing or hiking almost every day for two weeks. And then Alton went home to Illinois, and Chris went home to Indiana. The other fifty weeks of the year, they e-mailed whenever they wanted to—usually once or twice a month.

Now, if Chris had been his *only* friend? Then his mom bugging him would have made some sense. But he had other friends too—like Heather and Val.

They both lived right here in town *and* they both went to his school. The three of them had met last June in Maple Park near the post office—each of them had been searching for the same geocache.

Geocaching was one of Alton's favorite things to do with his map skills. It was a geeky kind of sport, and it had started in 2000—right after really accurate satellite Global Positioning System information became available to anyone with a

GPS receiver. Someone got the bright idea that it would be fun to hide little boxes or tins or bottles or jars, and then publish the GPS coordinates of these geocaches on a website. It was like a global game of hide-and-seek, and rules developed quickly. Most geocaches included a closed container with a log—a small notebook or paper—so a finder could sign it; and a lot of geocaches also contained little toys or trinkets called "swag"— bits of stuff that finders could take, and also add to.

Alton had a shoebox loaded with swag he had collected over the past two years—coins, a plastic clothespin, a little whistle, a braided key chain, a dog ID tag, a rubber spider—all kinds of small things. And whenever he took something from a geocache, he always left a blue rubber band behind—his own signature swag. Each rubber band was about a quarter of an inch wide and one inch around without being stretched. And on each rubber band, it looked like there was a black smudge. But stretch the band far enough, and a message would appear: SWAG COURTESY OF SIRMAPSALOT—which was Alton's geocaching nickname—his "handle." Alton got his hidden message onto the rubber band by stretching it to three times its length and then writing on it with a fine-point permanent marker.

Geocaching had gotten really popular very fast. And today? Within twenty-five miles of Harper's Grove, there were more than *seven hundred* geocaches, all of them hidden just in the last three years. And by one estimate, there were more than two and a half *million* active geocaches worldwide! Alton liked knowing that he was one of more than six million geocachers all over the world, fellow map nuts—including Val and Heather.

And in Maple Park on that day in June, the three of them had exchanged e-mail addresses and then, over the next few weeks, they'd decided to form a geocaching team to both hide and seek geocaches together. And during the summer, they'd become friends.

Except . . . they were all constantly competing, too. Because team-geocaching is like that—sort of like being crew members on the same pirate ship. Yes, you worked together to hunt for that next prize, but when it came down to sharing treasure, it was pretty much everyone for himself . . . or herself. Heather had made it clear from the start that she was as tough as any geo-pirate out there. Because if she got to a new cache before he or Val did, she didn't hand out any free clues. She'd just smile and say, "Go find it yourselves!"

So, yes, Alton already had some friends.

Still . . . he knew that a friend like Quint would be different.

And that was why Alton had decided to show Quint some of his best maps. Because if the guy thought some little doodles and sketches were so *epic*, then the maps he'd really worked on would probably stun him—maybe Quint would be so amazed that he would stop using slang for a minute or two.

And also, maybe then he'd have a new friend who lived in town and who went to his school— and who *wasn't* a map nut. Because he knew that was what his mom meant by her questions about finding new friends. She thought he spent way too much time messing with maps and geocaching and GPS devices—and he thought *she* spent way too much time watching funny cat videos on YouTube.

But when making friends with Quint started to feel like a very big deal—that was when Alton had gone that one stupid step too far. Because suddenly he wasn't just going to show Quint some of his best maps. No, he had decided to show the guy his folder of *secret* maps.

The folder itself wasn't fancy—just an ordinary

pocket folder that would fit inside a school note-book. And the maps in the folder weren't even big—the largest one was eleven inches high by seventeen inches wide with one fold down the middle. The rest of the maps were the size of ordinary printer paper.

He kept this folder hidden behind the book-case in his bedroom, where his mom or dad or his little sister would never think to look. He got it out only when he had a new map to add to it, and he always kept the folder at home.

Until yesterday morning.

And yesterday during social studies, he'd turned and looked Quint right in the eye and whispered, "Can you keep a secret?"

"A what?"

"Shhh! A secret—can you keep a secret?"

Quint's eyes had opened wide, and he'd nod-ded. "Yeah, *totally!*"

Alton said, "Okay, get a pass to the library for after lunch, and I'll meet you there. I've got something that will *astonish* you!"

He wasn't sure if Quint would even know that word, but apparently he did, because the two had met up around twelve fifteen. They went to a table near the back of the library.

Quint whispered, "Yo, I am so *stoked*, like, *wicked* psyched!"

Alton opened his folder and pulled out one of his favorite maps: "Miss Wheeling's Brain."

Which nearly caused a disaster, because Quint took one look and began laughing so hard that Alton was afraid his head would explode.

Which was an exaggeration, and Alton hated exaggerations almost as much as he hated slang.

But it truly was a huge blast of laughter, and it required a jab in Quint's ribs from Alton plus a frown and a very loud "Shhh!" from Mrs. Lomax to get Quint halfway under control again. Some sixth-grade girls at a nearby table turned and stared at them, curious about the commotion.

But Alton hadn't been surprised by Quint's reaction: a good map delivers a lot of information almost instantly, and if that information happens to be funny . . . *Boom!*

Still snorting a little, Quint had gasped, "This is totally *ill*—like, completely *sick*! How did you make this stuff up, dude?"

That question had forced Alton to give a short lecture: "Mapmakers don't make stuff up. They present facts. Because a map isn't really a map if it doesn't deal with facts."

And the fact was, after observing Miss Wheeling in class five days a week for the past two months, Alton had collected strong evidence that GOLDEN RETRIEVERS occupied a large portion of her mental territory—followed by CUPCAKES and her little brother, CARL—who also loved golden retrievers. Then came the CHICAGO BEARS, the METRIC SYSTEM, and HAWAIIAN VACATIONS.

One of the funniest parts of the drawing was the way he had surrounded the image of her brain with frizzy, puffy hair—obviously Miss Wheeling's hairdo. She had very curly hair, and Alton had seen her trying to comb it out when she came inside after recess or bus duty, especially when it was rainy or windy. She never looked happy about it.

Miss Wheeling was pretty good at her job, even though this was her first year of teaching. So, of course, *mostly* she talked about science and math, as Alton had explained in the legend on the map. As a bonus feature in the legend, Alton had included a short list of topics that Miss Wheeling had never mentioned in class even once: a boyfriend; a hobby; a book she liked; a TV show she liked; a movie she liked.

As he'd had to explain to Quint, the legend

lays out the limits of what a map presents. And within those limits, Alton was confident that this map gave an accurate peek into Miss Wheeling's twenty-three-year-old mind.

Quint had instantly agreed by laughing like crazy.

And . . . Quint's reaction was why Alton had kept this folder hidden away. Because his secret maps weren't about geography or politics or the environment. They were mostly about the kids and teachers at Harper School.

A couple of the maps were just silly, like the one that charted the popularity of Nike versus Reebok versus Adidas versus Converse versus Keds, and also high-tops versus low-tops. And he'd made a timeline-style map that showed what color shirts kids wore most on different days of the week—which was also kind of silly.

For maps like that, it wouldn't have mattered much if others knew about them—*except*, once those maps were out there? Then every kid and teacher would have figured out that Alton wasn't just studying his schoolwork every day—he was also studying *them*. And that would make collecting data in the future more difficult for him—which is why his maps about shoes and clothes and how often kids got haircuts, and his map of the location of twenty-nine different smells in the school went right into his secret folder.

But there was also a whole *other* category of maps—including "Miss Wheeling's Brain." These maps charted more personal stuff. Such as which girls liked which boys, and which boys liked which girls, and which girls hated which girls for liking certain boys. And how many sixth graders had parents who were divorced. And how often certain teachers smiled or frowned or got mad or yelled. And which tests kids cheated on the most—spelling, math, science, or social studies. And how many times Mrs. Buckley said "um" when she read the morning announcements over the PA, and which days of the week she said "um" the most. Alton had used Venn diagrams to make a popularity map of the cafeteria during sixth-grade lunch. And using contour lines like the kind on a hiking map, he had made a topographical height map of the sixth-grade class—from the lofty peak of Mount Wilson where Emma Wilson stood at five feet, eight inches, to the surrounding terrain where heights ranged from five feet, four inches, to four feet, six inches, and then down to the lowlands of Virden Valley—four feet, one inch, above level ground—which was where Cal Virden stood all by himself.

The maps were clever and accurate, and they were beautifully drawn. And some of them were sort of funny, and a few were *really* funny.

But Alton knew that the way he presented some of this more personal information? Some people would feel embarrassed—or maybe even feel like he was attacking them. Because some of these maps were more like cartoons than regular maps. Yes, he was still presenting facts, but by combining these particular facts with these particular drawings? Some people were definitely going to think he was trying to be mean—which wasn't what he'd been aiming for, not at all. He was just trying to be creative, trying some experiments with different kinds of map formats, trying to blend some ideas. These maps were like an artist's sketchbook, a place to mess around with new ideas. And he had meant to keep them private, like a diary.

Which is why he had always kept these maps hidden away—until yesterday, when he had used them to try to impress Quint . . . who had laughed so hard after seeing the very first map that Mrs. Lomax had immediately kicked them both out of the library.

And after school yesterday, when he'd gone to his cubby and discovered that the map folder was missing? For a few seconds there, Alton had felt like he was going to throw up. Right away he'd realized Quint must have taken the maps. Except, he didn't want to just walk up to the kid out at the bus lines and accuse him, not without proof. So Monday after school, he'd done nothing.

But late Monday night, as he lay in bed imagining those maps getting out for all the world to see, Alton had decided that he had to do a really careful search of both sixth-grade classrooms. Because maybe he had somehow left the folder in the desk he used in Mr. Troy's room today after lunch, or maybe he'd left it somewhere else—he didn't think so . . . but he had to check.

Lying there in bed, he knew he had to find a way to search Mr. Troy's room, and especially Quint's cubby. That would be risky, but if he found the folder, it would be worth all the dangers.

And then came the unannounced fire drill during homeroom on Tuesday. When that alarm sounded, Alton knew in a flash that *this* was his opportunity. And when everyone else hurried to line up, he dropped low to the floor over near the windows. In thirty seconds he was alone in the room, and a minute later the whole school was empty.

Fortunately, Mr. Troy had left his classroom open during the fire drill, but Alton's quick search of both sixth-grade rooms on Tuesday morning had turned up absolutely nothing.

So now he was still stuck with that queasiness in the pit of his stomach . . . plus a guilty feeling from having tricked Miss Wheeling—*and* having gotten her in trouble with the principal.

It was a huge mess.

A big pothole near County Road 2150 jolted him back into the present, and three minutes later, as the bus squealed to a stop at the mailbox across from his house, Alton made himself face an ugly fact: Quint Harrison had stolen his maps.

As he stood up and walked down the aisle and got off the bus, he ran through his reasoning.

Opportunity?

Yes. Quint knew where Alton stored his books and things, because the wooden cubbies along the back wall of Miss Wheeling's room were all labeled, and they were wide open—no doors. And Quint was in and out of that room all day.

Motive?

Yes. Since he and Quint had gotten kicked out of the library by Mrs. Lomax, the guy had only had the chance to look at one map . . . so certainly he would want to see more—*like, totally, dude!*

And maybe that had been Quint's original plan,

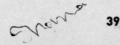

just to check out the other maps in the folder. After looking through all of them, Quint had probably realized how desperate Alton would be to get them back—he *must* have known that! But maybe the temptation to show them to others was too much. Maybe Quint had decided to show the maps to all his friends, to make himself even more popular—maybe he already had! Maybe he had already scanned them and posted all of them online!

That thought made Alton's stomach churn even worse. Because if those maps got spread around, it would be a long, long time before he would be making any new friends at school. Because on every map down in the lower right-hand corner, he had proudly written: *By Alton Ziegler.*

The bus roared away, and a chilly wind from the north rustled through the dry soybeans across the road from his house. But Alton didn't notice any of that. He had to get that folder back.

And since he hadn't found it at school, he was going to have to take this battle right to Quint's front door.

And the sooner he got there, the better.

CHAPTER SIX

HOT TOPICS

H i, Mom, we're home!"
Beth was Alton's little sister, and she sang out that announcement every school day afternoon.

"Hi, Beth—hi, Alton. I got some new yogurt today, all your favorite flavors. I'm in the middle of something, so I'll see you in about ten minutes, okay?"

Alton frowned and headed for the kitchen.

He was glad he'd have a little time before he had to answer twenty questions about his school day. His mom was a bookkeeper for three different businesses in the area, and she worked from home most days. She always made it a point to be there when Alton and his sister got home from school, and she always wanted to know everything.

He pulled open the refrigerator, and Beth was there next to him.

"Can you get me down a strawberry-banana, please?"

Alton started to hand her a cup of yogurt.

"And can you pull the foil off for me?"

He glared at her. "Should I go get a spoon and feed it to you too?"

Beth stared up at him. Her lower lip trembled and her eyes filled with tears.

Alton felt a sharp stab of shame. "Hey, I'm sorry, Bethie—here, I'll take off the foil. And don't cry—I'm just a big jerk, that's all." He opened the container and held it out to her.

Beth was in second grade, and she rode the bus with Alton every day. This afternoon he hadn't even noticed her. But she had noticed him.

She brushed at her eyes, and then smiled and took the yogurt. "It's okay, Alton. You're not a jerk. You're just sad today. I saw you frowning all the way home. What's the matter?"

"Nothing much. I just . . . lost something, that's all."

She brightened up. "I'm *really* good at finding things!"

Alton smiled. "I know you are, but I've got to find this thing on my own."

"Okay," she said. She ate a spoonful of yogurt, and then added "But if you need me to help, tell me. Because I don't want you to be sad."

Alton patted her on the head. "Thanks—that means a lot." And he meant it.

His mom called out, "Alton? Can you tell me why I just got a text from Heather addressed to you? On *my* phone?"

"Simple," he called back, his mouth full of yogurt. "Because *my* dumb little phone doesn't get texts, remember? If I had my own smartphone with a decent service plan, then I could get my own texts, like all the other sixth-grade kids do. And I'd always have a GPS receiver in my pocket, too."

This was a hot topic in the Ziegler home.

His mom stood at the kitchen doorway now, her phone in her hand.

"*All* the other sixth graders text with smartphones? All of them?"

"Okay," Alton said, "seventy-two percent of them do—I took a survey. So that's almost three-fourths. And no matter what the statistics are, I should definitely have one of my own. I should."

Beth said, "Well, if Alton gets a new phone, *I* should get one too!"

Alton said, "You don't even have a regular cell phone—and you know the percentage of second graders who have their own phones? It's about *zero*. So just be quiet, okay? This is between Mom and me."

"Fine," said Beth. "But you can forget about me helping you find that thing you lost." And for emphasis she stuck a huge spoonful of yogurt into her mouth and turned her back to him.

"What thing?" his mom said. "What did you lose?"

As casually as possible Alton said, "Just some maps I made. But I think a guy in my social studies class picked them up. And I'm going to ride my bike over to his house in a little while and get them back."

His mom said, "Say, speaking of maps, I turned in an article to the *Observer* about using computer tax programs, and when I saw Mrs. Girard, she asked me if you might be interested in making a map about the town's history. She remembers that map you sent her about the migrating birds. She's planning a feature in February about how the town has changed from 1903 to the present day."

Glad that the conversation had shifted, Alton said, "I could do that. . . . Do you think she'll pay me?"

"Well . . . I think she's hoping you would do it for free—you didn't get paid for the last map."

"Mom, I was in second grade then, and I drew that map with crayons. This one would be a lot harder, with tons more detail—it would be a real map."

"*I'm* in second grade," said Beth, "and *I* make real maps all the time!"

"Of course you do, sweetie," her mom said. Then to Alton, "You should call her up. If you're reasonable, she'd probably be happy to pay you something."

"Okay," said Alton. "Can I borrow your phone?"

His mom stared. "You're calling her right now?"

"No," Alton said. "I have to text Heather back. I know she wants to go out geocaching, and I can't this afternoon. And I don't want to call her, because she'll argue and try to talk me into it."

With a sigh, his mom handed over her phone. But she stood there with her hand out, waiting for him to finish the text.

When he gave it back to her, he said, "I'm going upstairs and do some homework before I ride over to Quint's house to get my maps."

"Quint? Quint who?"

"Is he a quintuplet?" asked Beth.

"No, he's not a quintuplet," Alton said. And to his mom, he said, "His name is Quint Harrison, and he lives in town on the west side. So it's a short ride. And I'll wear my helmet and I'll have all my lights on, and I won't be gone for more than half an hour, okay?"

"All right. But let me know when you leave."

"I will," he said.

"And will you just ask him if he's a quintuplet?" said Beth. "Please?"

Alton smiled at her as he picked up his backpack. "Sure. I'll ask him—I promise."

CHAPTER SEVEN

NAVIGATION

As Alton rode due east on County Road 1145, the low afternoon sun threw his shadow way out ahead of him. By his calculation, each spin of his bicycle wheels moved him 6.98 feet closer to his destination. He was traveling at about thirteen miles per hour, and the total trip was only about two and a half miles. So this was going to be a pretty short ride—no more than seven minutes.

Alton loved his bike. It had twenty-one gears, and it had skinny tires that held a hundred pounds of air pressure, so pedaling was easy. Living in the flattest county in Illinois also helped with the pedaling. And with land so flat and nearly all the roads running either north–south or east–west, it was almost impossible to get lost—which was a feeling he liked.

At the moment, he was navigating a very simple course:

At end of driveway, turn left onto CR 1145 North.

Ride east for 1.13 miles.

Turn left onto CR 2150 East.

Ride north for 0.78 miles.

Turn right onto West Jackson Street.

Ride east 0.63 miles to 5233 West Jackson Street, a house on the right.

And at 5233 West Jackson, Alton was planning to walk up to the front door and ask for Quint.

He wanted his arrival to be a complete surprise. There was no guarantee Quint would be home, but by planning to arrive at five o'clock, he felt good about his chances.

As he signaled and made a smooth left turn onto County Road 2150, Alton got a familiar sensation—like he was rolling across the surface of a map as big as the Earth.

Which was a pretty goofy idea. The map of Illinois on the wall in his room showed a shrunken image of the whole state, including all the roads and towns and rivers and railroads and state parks and airports and everything, and it was drawn so that one inch on the map represented twelve miles on the ground. But if that map were redrawn so that one inch on the map was the same as one inch on the ground? Then the *map* of Illinois would be the same size as Illinois itself!

To hang *that* map up, you'd need a wall as big as the sky, and to look at it, you'd have to fly around in a helicopter or something. And if you spread that full-scale map out onto the ground, then the only way to use it would be to do what he was doing right now—travel around on it! Which would defeat the whole idea of a geographical map. Because a map was a symbol, a small image of a big area, and it was supposed to let you see how to get from one location to another one *without* having to actually go there. . . .

A huge grain truck shot past him doing about fifty-five, and the sharp blast of air and fumes caught Alton off guard. His front wheel wobbled, and the bike veered toward the shoulder, but he tapped both brakes and managed to stay on the blacktop.

Alton stopped thinking about imaginary maps and paid attention to real road conditions.

Two minutes later the farmland stopped, and the small town of Harper's Grove began, with the streets carving the land into square blocks, and with the houses all numbered and arranged neatly, side-by-side.

And three minutes after that, Alton turned into the driveway at 5233 West Jackson. He rode right onto the front walk, laid his bike on the grass, pulled off his helmet, marched up the steps to the porch, put his finger on the doorbell . . . and froze.

What do I say?

He could start with something like, *There's a problem we need to talk about, Quint.* Or *Listen, I know you took my maps, so hand 'em over!* Or . . . maybe he needed to sound even tougher than that: *Hey, hand over those maps right now, or I'm making a map of your puny, slang-infested brain, and I'm going to paste copies of it all over the school!*

But Alton couldn't imagine himself saying any of those things. He gulped and lifted his finger off the doorbell, then took a step backward.

I've got to get out of here!

Before he could move, the door whipped open. Quint was all smiles. "*Dude!* Like, how did you get here? Oh, wait—*duh*! A map! You *totally* used a map, didn't you?"

"Um . . . yeah, I—I did," Alton stammered. "I used a map."

"So, like, how come you came over?"

Alton looked Quint right in the eye. "You don't know why I'm here? You have no idea?"

"No," said Quint. "Why?"

Alton's own failures as a liar had made him an expert at spotting the lies of others. And in Quint's wide-open face he saw nothing, no hint of dishonesty.

"So . . . you don't know where my maps are, the ones I had in the library on Monday?"

Quint shook his head, and then his eyes suddenly narrowed. "*Whoa*—like, did you think *I* took them? Like, that I *stole* them? Dude, I would never do that!"

Alton felt his face getting warm. "Well, it's just that I had to ask you, because I haven't been able to find them . . . and I've looked everywhere. Um . . . and I thought you might know something. . . . That's all."

Quint nodded slowly. "I totally get that. But I haven't seen 'em, not since Monday." Then he grinned. "'Miss Wheeling's Brain'—that map is *epic*! Hey, come on in, okay? I've got to ask you something."

Alton was surprised by the invitation, but he followed Quint inside.

The TV was on in the living room, and Quint aimed his thumb at a girl on the couch who looked like she was sixteen or seventeen.

"That's my sister. Hey, Liz, this is Al—I mean, Alton. From school."

The girl glanced up for half a second and gave Alton a tiny nod.

A voice called out, "Bring 'Alton from school' into the kitchen and introduce him to your mom and me!"

At the kitchen doorway, Quint said, "This is my mom and dad. And this is Alton Ziegler. "

Quint's mom was sitting at the table in front of a laptop, and his dad was standing at the stove, stirring a big pot of something that smelled like stew or maybe soup.

Alton felt awkward, but he managed to smile at them. "Glad to meet you."

"It's good to meet you, too," his mom said. "Do you live nearby?"

"Not too far," Alton said, "pretty much straight west on County Road 1145. I rode my bike over."

"You know, I think we met your mom and dad at the PTO book fair last year. And you have a sister—am I remembering that right?"

Alton nodded. "My little sister, Beth—she's in second grade this year."

"Sounds nice," Quint said. "Wanna trade?"

His sister called from the living room, "I heard that, Squint."

He called back, "You were *supposed* to hear it, Lizard."

"That's enough," his mom said.

Quint said, "Listen, Mom, I've got to ask Alton about some school stuff, okay?"

She wasn't going to be hurried. "Can you stay for dinner, Al?"

"Um, thanks, but I've got to ride back home. It's a school night."

"Maybe another time, all right?"

"Sure . . . thanks."

"This way," Quint said, and he led Alton back through the living room and up the stairs near the front door.

His bedroom was the first door on the left. Alton didn't know what he'd been expecting, but it wasn't what he saw. Because Quint's room was loaded with books. Also model trains. And plastic dinosaurs. Plus a collection of rocks and a deadly looking hammer lying alongside four or five books about geology and minerals.

On top of a bookcase Alton spotted seven pocketknives carefully laid out in a line, and some of them looked old. And next to the knives there was a bunch of rusty railroad spikes. He also saw a hiking stick leaning in a corner. The bed was a big mess and there were clothes and shoes all over the place, but this was *not* the room of a kid who vegged out in front of video games or sat around watching Nick at Nite reruns all the time. Which was sort of how Alton had pictured Quint's life, because of all the slang.

Quint was leaning over a large table that he apparently used as his desk.

"Dude, check this out. I started making a list of the railroads that used to run through Illinois, and then I found out about all these abandoned railroad beds. I know this map is super-lame, but it'd be awesome if you had any ideas about jazzing it up."

Alton took a look. What Quint had so far was a sheet of plain paper where he'd traced a basic outline of Illinois. Six or seven major cities had been placed in roughly the correct locations, and then he'd used half a dozen colored markers to draw in different stretches of abandoned railroad tracks. With a fine-point black pen he had written a little about each one. He was getting his information from six or seven other maps that he'd printed out from several websites.

"Wow—I had no idea there were so many abandoned tracks around!"

"Yeah, I know—crazy, right? So far it's, like, more than a thousand miles of track in Illinois, and I keep finding even more—it blows my mind!"

Alton's mind was blown too. Racing through a big collection of new information always made him feel sort of lost—and *that* always made him want to get everything organized on a map. Because this information could be laid out in a lot of different ways. First of all, there would have to be a comprehensive list of—

Quint interrupted his thoughts. "See this bit here that I drew in green?" He put his finger on the map at a line that looked like it was a little south of Champaign. "My dad and I hiked that this summer—nine miles of the old Wabash Railroad."

Alton nodded toward the bookcase. "Is that where you got the spikes?"

"Totally." Quint went and picked one up. "So . . . like, a hundred and fifty years ago, some guy with a humongous hammer pounded this thing into a chunk of wood to hold the rails steady. And you know who rode on those rails? Abraham Lincoln! Way cool, huh?"

"Yes, it is," said Alton. "That's pretty amazing."

"Here." Quint handed the spike to him. "You want it? I've got loads of 'em."

"Really?" Alton said. "Thanks!"

"So, check this out," said Quint. "I already asked Mr. Troy if I could make a project out of this stuff for my fall report, and he said it was cool. So, like, how about we both work on it?"

The mention of school reminded Alton why he'd come here in the first place.

"Um, sure," he said. "That'd be great . . . except, first I've really got to find those missing maps."

"Dude, I'm totally gonna help you with that— it'll be like we're private detectives—*The Case of the Missing Maps*. And we're gonna nail the crooks who snagged 'em—like, *wham!*"

Alton didn't know what to say. Did he really want to team up with a kid he barely knew, a guy with a language disorder? Still, some help wouldn't be bad—and Quint was clearly much smarter than Alton had thought he was.

"Um . . . sure," he said. "That might be good. But right now? I've got to ride home before it gets any darker."

When they got downstairs, Quint's dad heard them at the door. "So long, Alton," he called from the kitchen.

And Quint's mom added, "It was nice to meet you—hope you can come visit again."

"Thanks," he called back. "It was nice to meet you, too."

Quint's sister was still on the couch, and her eyes never left the TV.

They went outside, and Alton picked up his bike off the lawn.

"Hey, you know what?" said Quint. "First you should make a map of everywhere you took your maps—a maps map, get it?" Then he said, "Here," and handed Alton a slip of paper. "That's my cell number so we can text."

"Right," Alton said. He felt too embarrassed to tell Quint that his phone didn't have a text plan.

He put the railroad spike and the slip of paper in his jacket pocket, then pulled on his helmet and turned on his bike lights.

Quint said, "Listen, I'm glad you came over—even though you thought I jacked your maps."

"Yeah," Alton said, "sorry about that." And then he remembered something. "This is going to sound really strange, but you're not a quintuplet, right?"

"What?! Course not."

Alton grinned. "I promised my sister I'd ask."

Quint laughed. "Little kids are *wicked* cool!"

Alton said, "Well, see you tomorrow . . . and thanks again for the spike."

"Don't mention it. Later, dude."

"Later," said Alton.

Coasting down the driveway, Alton realized he'd just replied with the slangiest thing he'd ever said.

And actually, it felt kind of . . . normal.

CHAPTER EIGHT

CONTACT

One question stomped around inside Alton's head all Tuesday night, and it was still there pacing back and forth when he woke up on Wednesday morning: If Quint didn't take his folder . . . then who did? And how was Alton even going to know where to start looking for the answer?

It turned out that the answer came looking for him.

As he put away his backpack and gym shoes before homeroom, Alton spotted a plain white envelope lying on the top shelf of his cubby. The envelope wasn't sealed, and when he lifted the flap and looked inside, his heart almost stopped. It was a bunch of cut-out letters pasted onto a slip of white paper:

**iS someThing missing?
do whaT uT toLd—or else.
u'Ll heaR fRm me**

Alton slapped the envelope shut and pressed it between his palms. His heart began thumping and his mouth felt dry.

He glanced around—no one was looking at him.

Standing there next to his cubby, he tried to think, tried to process the message, tried to grasp what it meant. And then he realized he'd better try to breathe.

He sucked in a quick breath, then peeked at the message again. Right away he saw it wasn't really cut-out letters—it was a computer typeface that was made to look that way.

There were three parts to the message: a question, a threat, and a promise.

Alton looked at the clock—four minutes until the bell. He stuffed the envelope into his back pocket and hurried into the hall, scanning the faces to his left and right—no Quint.

He went to Mr. Troy's doorway, spotted Quint, then walked right into the room. Trying to seem casual, he went up to a group of guys, nodded at everyone, and said, "Hey, Quint, you know that . . . project? Um, can we talk about it for a second?"

"Ab-so-tively."

Alton said, "I mean . . . over in Miss Wheeling's room?"

Quint nodded. "No prob." Then to the other guys he said, "Later."

When they were in the hall, Alton said, "Look at this, but do *not* react, okay? Just look."

He took out the envelope and lifted the flap so Quint could see inside. Quint's eyes popped open wide, and Alton quickly jammed the envelope back into his pocket.

"Whoa! Like . . . *whoa!*" Quint whispered, "You know what that is, right? It's a ransom note, like . . . *totally!*"

"I know!"

Quint looked over his shoulder. "The dude who sent that could be scoping us out *right now*! Or . . . it might be a *dudette*! So, like, what're you gonna do?"

Alton shrugged. "Not much I *can* do. I think I just have to wait. Until the kidnapper makes a demand."

"Kidnapper?" Quint shook his head. "Nuh-uh, no way, dude. What we've got here is a *map*napper!"

"Right," Alton said, and he smiled, even though he didn't feel like it.

Quint looked around again. "So, here's a brain wave—ready? You shouldn't show me anything you get from the mapnapper, not so anybody could see you showing it to me—get it? Then I can be a secret watcher. Someone'll be watching *you*, and I'll be watching for the *watcher*. Cool, huh?"

"Good idea," Alton said. "But . . . what about working on the railroads project?"

"We can totally still do that—which gives me another idea!" Quint looked around, and then in a voice about six times louder than it needed to be, he said, "So, that'll be cool, Alton. And we can talk to Mr. Troy about this railroad stuff during social studies. And we can work on it some more at lunch, okay?"

Quint was a terrible actor, but Alton played along.

He nodded, and in a voice almost as loud as Quint's, he said, "Yeah, I've got some ideas for getting all the information organized."

Alton was a bad actor too.

Their scene needed an ending, so Quint said, "This'll be great—see you later . . . dude."

"Right . . . so long."

Alton went back to Miss Wheeling's home-room feeling kind of dumb.

But he hoped their dopey little scene in the hall had worked anyway. It might be good if Quint could be a secret watcher.

He went to his cubby again to get his things for first and second periods—and he looked on the top shelf. No envelope.

Sitting down at his desk, he felt awkward and self-conscious, sort of the way he felt at his own birthday parties. Because whoever had his maps was probably watching him. At this very moment, *he* was the center of someone's attention, like a bug under a microscope . . . or sort of like the kids and teachers he had watched when he was gathering information for some of those maps in his folder—except none of them had been aware that someone was studying them. Which made it completely different from this . . . or at least mostly different . . . right? He wasn't sure.

The one thing he *was* sure about? He would be getting another message from this mapnapper. And he hoped it would happen soon.

It did.

CHAPTER NINE

HOW THIS WORKS

It was second period, and Alton was sitting in Mr. Troy's room. He was supposed to be reading a story to get ready for a comprehension exercise, but instead he was using a scrap of paper to sketch a map of where his maps had been—which was one of Quint's ideas. And he was racking his memory to be sure he got the order right.

When Mrs. Lomax had kicked them out of the library on Monday, he'd grabbed everything, and then he and Quint had walked directly outside to the playground—but they'd only stayed there about three minutes. And then he'd gone to his homeroom to drop off his book bag and get his gym shoes. And that was it.

So . . . who could have known that he'd had that folder of maps in his backpack, which he had put in his cubby? It *had* to have been someone who was in the library. Maybe someone . . . And then he remembered. *Of course!* That group of girls, the one sitting a couple tables away! The girls were *right there*—and when Quint started laughing like a hyena, they'd all turned and stared at him!

But Alton couldn't remember any names—or even their faces, not clearly.

He made a note to ask Quint about that during third-period math. . . . No, he'd have to wait until lunchtime and maybe pass him a note about it. Because they couldn't give anybody hints that they were working together on this.

He glanced at the clock and saw that he'd better hurry up and read the assigned story. He folded his sketch and tucked it into his reading book—and that was when he noticed it.

Just half an inch was sticking out of the pages near the back of the book, but there was no mistaking what it was: a white envelope!

Alton didn't gasp, but his breathing got fast and shallow. He wanted to look all around the room, to study every kid's face until he spotted the telltale smile or twitch or glance that would give the mapnapper away.

But he didn't do that.

He laid his reading book flat on the desk and slowly pulled the envelope toward him, out from between the pages. It was the same normal business-size envelope, and again, the flap wasn't sealed.

Holding the envelope close to his stomach, he lifted the flap and peeked:

heres how this works—
1. u get an order.
2. do it—and u get 1 map back.
And if u don't?
all ur maps go public.

Alton felt his face heating up. This wasn't just a case of kidnapped maps anymore—no, this person was saying, *Do what I say, or else!* This was blackmail!

And there was more—on a second slip of paper:

first order—
stop wearing map shirts
starting after 9am today.

What?

Wear different shirts? Starting *today*?! Unbelievable!

There was a lost-and-found bin in Mr. Ludlow's office . . . so if he just slopped a bunch of water down the front of his New York City Subway T-shirt, he was sure the gym teacher would let him pick out something else to wear.

But that wasn't the real problem.

The real problem was that there were at least ten other maps in his folder! And if *this* was the first order, there was no telling what might come later on.

But what can I do?

Alton did the only thing he *could* do: He gritted his teeth and kept thinking.

But as he began his reading assignment, he made a promise to himself: *I will figure out who's doing this, and once I've got all my maps back? There's going to be payback!*

CHAPTER TEN

ESCALATION

Quint answered instantly: "Kelley, Jaclyn, Catherine, and Elena."

Alton stared at him. Then he said, "You're *one hundred percent sure* that those are the girls who were in the library at lunchtime on Monday?"

Quint raised one eyebrow and smiled. "I *always* notice the girls, dude . . . because *they* always notice me."

They were whispering to each other. It was seventh period, and Mr. Troy had given them permission to work on the railroads project at the back of his room for the last ten minutes of class.

Alton decided not to comment on Quint's statement about girls.

"Okay . . . ," he said. "So, any opinions about these girls you noticed? Do you think one of them could be sending me the notes?"

Quint shrugged. "I know their *names*, dude—it's not like we talk much or anything. But they're *totally* the ones who saw me laughing, and they must have seen you put your stuff away. So, yeah, it's possible—I mean, who else could it be?"

Alton kept pressing for an answer. "But if you had to pick one who *might* try something like this, which one would it be?"

"Hmm—whoever's doing this is kinda smart . . . so it's prolly not gonna be Jaclyn. And she would have to be pretty tough, so that cuts out Kelley. And it has to be someone with a sense of humor, too. So if it's really one of those four girls, it'd have to be Elena—yeah, Elena . . . totally."

Alton nodded slowly. "Funny, tough, and smart . . . I can see that. I got paired up with Elena to do a report on Russia when we were in fourth grade. She made me do all the work, and she made fun of how hard I worked on my map—and then she told me how to make it better."

Quint smiled. "Yup, that's what she's like."

Alton wasn't smiling. "Elena . . . that makes sense—because on one of my maps? I kind of made fun of how she likes to wear strong perfume."

Nodding wisely, Quint said, "Yeah, that'd prolly be enough to set her off. Last year, over at the high school? Some guy made fun of my sister's shoes. Let's just say that the dude wished he hadn't. For about a month." Then he added, "Of course, all four girls *could* be in on this together, and Elena's just the mastermind."

They were quiet for a second, then Quint said, "But really, would it even matter if we knew for sure it was Elena—or all of them? *Somebody* has your maps, and unless you follow these stupid orders, that *somebody* is gonna drop the bomb. But, c'mon, like, how bad could that be? Why not just call the bluff and let all the maps go public? There's a little boom-boom action, and then it's over. Simple. It's just a bunch of maps, right?"

The look of severe pain on Alton's face stopped Quint cold.

"So . . . what am missing here, dude?" he whispered.

Alton chose his words carefully. "Um . . . those maps? If they got passed around without any explanation at all? Some people would get . . . upset— like Elena did, except probably worse. Really offended. Maybe furious. And it might be a *lot* of people." Alton paused. "Maybe even you."

"*Me?* I'm on your maps somewhere? *Cool!* Tell me!"

"You know what a Venn diagram is?" Alton asked.

"Ab-so-tively . . . a buncha circles, right? And they overlap. Like, each circle represents a set, and where they overlap, it means they have shared elements."

"Exactly," Alton said, reminding himself again that Quint was really smart. "Well, I made a popularity map of the cafeteria during sixth-grade lunch, and I used Venn diagrams. Except the Venn circles aren't just made with lines—I made the circles using words. And you? You're in the very center circle, which is where the most popular kids are. And the circle around you and your friends is made up of words like *cool, fantastic, so popular, top dogs, check us out, we are wonderful, look at us, dream on, we love ourselves, cute* AND *handsome, howdy, losers*—stuff like that."

Quint made a face. "Kinda harsh, dude." He looked at Alton. "So . . . that's what you think I'm like?"

Alton shook his head. "No, definitely not . . . I mean, not anymore. But I used to, just a few days ago. Because me? My name is in a circle way out on the edge with a bunch of other geeky kids, and the circle around our names is made up of words

73

like, *not really, just barely here, pretty much invisible, never mind, just watching, don't mind us, who would even notice* . . . Things like that. And from way out there, it's all guesswork about the popular kids. Because your circle and my circle? They never cross—they don't even come close."

"*Whoa!* That is deep, dude . . . *deep.*" Quint thought some more, then said, "But I gotta say, you've got some stuff wrong . . . seriously. I mean, I prolly *look* like I'm popular and everything, but, like, it's not like I'm actually pals with those kids. We just hang out at school . . . and talk and laugh and stuff. From across the room it *looks* like I belong in that circle, but all I really am is a visitor." He held up his hand, and his eyes got wide. "Wait—this is a major brain wave! *Maybe* all those maps of yours really *need* to get out there! To make kids think. Like, maybe it's your mission, dude—like . . . Karma . . . or something. To make kids think about stuff like this! Blast all those maps out there, and let 'er rip!"

Alton shook his head. "Trust me, that would not be good."

"How come?"

So Alton took a deep breath. And then he told Quint about the which-kids-like-and-hate-which-other-kids maps; and about the divorced-parents map; and about the which-teachers-yell-and-frown-most map; and about the how-many-times-does-the-principal-say-"um" map; and about the sixth-graders'-heights map; and about the which-tests-get-cheated-on-most map. And also about the trips-to-the-bathroom-compared-with-cafeteria-menus map; and about the twenty-nine-smells-around-the-school map. And, of course, "Miss Wheeling's Brain."

When Alton stopped describing the maps, Quint looked a little stunned. "I get what you mean. If all *that* got loose at once, it might be pretty rough."

"I know," said Alton. "I know. Because it's like I was making up map cartoons, just messing around. I wasn't going to show them to anyone. And I *shouldn't* have shown any to you."

"So . . . how come you did?"

Before Alton could reply, Quint said, "*Ohhh*—I get it! You pegged me as popular and cool and amazingly wonderful . . . instead of me *actually* being a half-popular, semi-nerdy collector of dinosaur dolls and railroad spikes. . . . Is that about right?"

Alton smiled sheepishly. "Exactly. Guilty as

charged. And now I'm paying for my crime."

Quint grinned. "Well, on the bright side? *That* is a seriously *excellent* shirt you have on!"

Alton acted like he was going to slug Quint on the arm, but he pulled back. The shirt Mr. Ludlow had taken out of the gym's lost-and-found bin was a fluorescent green sweatshirt with its sleeves cut off right up to the armpits.

Alton shook his head. "I have never owned anything this color in my life—except maybe a piece of gum."

"I bet the mapnapper's getting a big laugh about it!"

Alton said, "Hey—you know what? Guess who I spotted pointing at this shirt and laughing, right after gym."

Quint shrugged. "Who?"

"Elena!"

"No *way*!"

"Shh!" Alton glanced around, and Mr. Troy was frowning at them. "Look, we need to actually do some work on your railroad stuff—and we've only got five minutes left. Did you bring that map you started?"

"Yup." Quint pulled a clipboard out of his backpack. "It's right . . . *whoa!*"

Alton saw what Quint saw—a plain white business envelope, stuck under the big silver clip.

"So . . . ," Alton said slowly, "it looks like we can stop trying to pretend that you're not part of the maps recovery squad."

Quint nodded. "Yeah, my cover's blown . . . totally."

Alton said, "Open it."

Quint's hands shook a little as he pulled the message from the envelope. They both read it silently.

Nice shirt, Alton—mapless is good.
and 1 map is returned—in Quint's cubby—lots more to go.
Next order:
Before homeroom tomorrow, tell mrs. Buckner she saw um too much. have fun with that.

Quint whispered, "You've gotta tell *that* to the principal? *Ouch!* How're you gonna do it?"

Alton took the message and tucked it back in its envelope. "Not sure," he said grimly. "But I'll find a way . . . because I have to."

Quint said, "This is prolly gonna sound sorta mean, dude . . . but listen, can I come with you to the principal's office . . . and watch?"

Alton smiled. "Sure. I might need a witness in case she slams me over the head with her briefcase."

"Cool! Count me in!"

But as the bell rang and he gathered up his things, Alton was pretty sure that tomorrow morning's chat with Mrs. Buckley would *not* be cool.

At all.

CHAPTER ELEVEN

UNAVOIDABLE

I am starving!

But before Alton had taken two steps toward the kitchen, he caught himself. Because *that* was a huge exaggeration, and he hated exaggerations. He had *never* been starving—or anywhere even close to starving—not one day of his whole life.

There was a large glass bowl of cut-up oranges and apples and bananas in the fridge, and he could tell his mom had prepared the fruit within the past hour, because the bananas hadn't started turning brown yet.

He had both hands around the bowl when Beth said, "Can you reach me down a blueberry yogurt?"

"Sure," he said. He let go of the fruit, got the yogurt, and without being asked, he pulled the foil off the container and handed it to Beth with a smile.

"Thank you."

"You are so welcome."

Alton put the fruit on the table, grabbed a soup spoon from the drawer, sat down, peeled the plastic wrap off the bowl, and dug in—it was *so* good!

He was on his fifth mouthful when his mom walked in and said, "Guess what? I—" She stopped and stared. "Alton! Did you really think that *entire* bowl of fruit was just for you? Honestly—you'd think we lived in a cave somewhere. Get a cereal bowl, serve yourself a reasonable portion, and put the rest back in the refrigerator. *Now*."

Alton said, "Oh—right. Sorry. It's just that I was star—really hungry."

Once he was sitting down again, his mom said, "I was just starting to tell you that I got a new phone today."

Alton's mouth dropped open, and he forgot all about the fruit—some of which was there in plain view, half chewed.

"I got a new a phone? *A new phone?!* That's amazing! That's—"

"Hold it," his mom interrupted. "You didn't hear me, Alton. I said *I* got a new phone. But it does mean that I now have an *old* phone, and your dad and I have decided that you can use it. And the woman at the phone store got it set up, so all you need to do is plug in the data card from the phone you have now. And *immediately* after you do that, you have to call Heather and Val and Christopher and tell each of them to *stop* sending texts to *my* number, all right?"

And she reached out and handed Alton the phone—her old one.

He took it and held it with both hands, as if she might suddenly change her mind and try to wrestle it away from him.

"This is *so* great, Mom! Really, this is perfect. . . . Thanks!" And he jumped out of his chair and gave her a hug—still holding the phone tightly.

Beth's eyes got huge. "So . . . now *I* can have *Alton's* old phone, right?"

Her mom shook her head. "No, dear—I'm sorry. Not until you're in fourth grade. That's our rule."

"It's a *stupid* rule!"

Alton had to smile, even though he felt a little sorry for Beth. Because he knew that the argument she had just started was going to last for at least two more years.

Alton gobbled the rest of his fruit, then left the kitchen, trotting up the stairs and into his room.

He already knew his mom's phone inside and out—he was sure he understood it a lot better than she did. It was almost two years old, but it had a big, bright touch screen, good control buttons, and a decent GPS app, which was already installed and was almost as accurate as the hand-held GPS unit he'd been using for geocaching over the two years—and the antenna on this phone pulled in satellite signals strong and clear.

It took him less than a minute to insert his SIM card and restart the phone. And there they were, all his contacts—which weren't very many. But now it was official—this phone was *his*!

He was excited about the phone, and he had fun over the next half hour getting it set up just the way he wanted it. But tomorrow morning's meeting with Mrs. Buckley hung there in his mind like a large gray cloud.

He opened up the Google Earth app on the phone and messed with the settings. Then he moved the image until it showed the view from high above the town of Harper's Grove. Then he zeroed in on the roof of his school. He knew just where the principal's office was, there at the front, near the driveway. When he had the image centered correctly, he wrote down the latitude and longitude on a yellow note card.

It was kind of a dumb thing to do, but seeing that familiar-looking set of numbers made him feel better. Now he knew *exactly* where he would be sitting right before homeroom tomorrow.

But he had no idea what he'd say. How do you tell somebody like Mrs. Buckley that she says "um" too much? It was an impossible assignment.

But then he had a good thought: How would Elena or her pals or anybody else ever know *what* he was saying to the principal? Yes, someone could tell if he talked with Mrs. Buckley just by looking into the office. But they'd never know what he'd actually said to her—not unless they were right there in the room!

Then a horrible thought hit, and it almost took his breath away: The only other kid who *was* going to be there inside the principal's office was Quint—who had specifically *asked* if he could come along! So . . . was Quint in on this plot after all? Was he just a really fantastic liar? Was he the mastermind, putting together this huge practical joke and sharing it with all his friends?

Look at me! Alton thought. *I'm going completely crazy about this! Quint's a good guy—I'm sure he is!*

But his doubts about Quint wouldn't go away—not completely. And even having a smartphone of his very own didn't make him feel better.

Unless he wanted to risk having his maps get loose and maybe hurt a lot of people's feelings, he had to accept the idea that *somehow* the map-napper would be able to check up on him, would *somehow* know whether he had talked with Mrs. Buckley about her "um"-ing.

Alton put down his phone and picked up the yellow note card from his desk. He stared at the GPS coordinates he had copied down.

The principal's office was tomorrow morning's special destination, and there was no way to avoid it.

CHAPTER TWELVE

UM . . . A MIRACLE?

Alton Ziegler wondered if all principals' offices looked like Mrs. Buckley's office. He had no idea. In his whole life, this was the only principal's office he had ever seen.

And Alton suddenly wished that he was on a long car trip so that he could stop at every elementary school in every single city and town all across America. Because then he could take a picture of *every* principal's office. And then he could map all the information . . . like, how many pictures or posters were hung on the walls, how many photos of kids or pets or husbands or wives sat on the desks. . . . And was there a state flag *and* a US flag displayed in all those other offices too?

He could count how many principals sat on leather chairs, on cloth chairs, on wooden chairs, or on fancy steel-and-plastic chairs, like the one behind Mrs. Buckley's desk. And he could count the number of extra chairs in each principal's office—there were six here, all of them with square steel frames and worn cloth cushions . . . which reminded him that he had actually been hoping the chairs would have steel frames, because he had made a goofy geocaching plan with steel chairs in mind—all of which only distracted him from his observations for about five seconds.

He sat in the chair to the left of the principal's desk, and Quint sat in the chair on the right, and then there were four more chairs around a small table over in a corner.

And looking at that corner, Alton decided that this office was a square—about fifteen feet on each side. If he got to visit all those *other* offices? He could see which ones were square and which ones were rectangular—maybe there were some other shapes out there, like circles or ovals, maybe even a hexagon or two.

He could also learn how many offices had solid walls and doors, and how many had glass walls and doors. Because Mrs. Buckley had windows facing outdoors and windows facing the office and windows facing the hallway. All that glass made her office feel like a fishbowl. And he and Quint had been sitting in that fishbowl in front of her desk for three minutes now, because that's where the school secretary had told them to wait.

Alton caught a glimpse of himself reflected in the window behind the big desk. His gray T-shirt had a plain front—no map. Elena or one of her gang was probably waiting outside homeroom to check and be sure he was obeying her order. He clenched his teeth so hard, his jaw hurt.

That girl is going to wish she'd never started this!

And then Alton remembered—*he* was the one who had started this when he couldn't resist showing that map to Quint.

"Yo," Quint whispered, "I think this tagalong was a big mistake. Maybe I should disappear, huh?"

Alton looked sideways at him. That question actually made him happy, because it proved Quint wasn't part of some scheme to hear what he said to the principal.

"If you want to leave, sure. No sense in both of us getting in trouble. You can go."

Quint never got the chance.

"Good morning, boys."

Mrs. Buckley swept in, dropped a hat and gloves on the desk, and sat down in her chair. She swayed backward and then forward as she leaned onto her desk and smiled at Quint and then at Alton. She still had on her coat.

"Mrs. Ashton said you needed to talk with me. I've got only a minute before the last bus arrives, but I'll try to help. What's this about?"

Alton gulped, and then said, "Um, I wanted to ask you a question, Mrs. Buckley."

Faster than the speed of light, in that tiny fraction of a second after the sentence left his mouth, Alton panicked.

I'm here to ask her why she says um *so much, and what's the first word I just said?* Um!

But even faster, an idea took hold.

He gulped again and said, "Um, I wanted to ask you something, and it's sort of a weird question. Because, um, sometimes when I have to talk, and when I kind of get stuck? I say 'um.' And I noticed that . . . um, during the announcements in the morning? Um . . . you say it too. And . . . I was wondering if you know why you do that . . . um, why you say 'um' a lot?"

Mrs. Buckley's face turned bright red, so red that for a second Alton thought she was going to yell at him so loud that all the windows around them would shatter and collapse into glittering heaps.

But then he saw it. She wasn't mad—she was embarrassed.

Mrs. Buckley cleared her throat. "Well . . . that's a very perceptive question, Alton. And, um . . . all I can tell you is that I've been aware of this . . . problem for many years, and . . . I'm getting better at . . . keeping my words flowing . . . without feeling like I need to fill . . . every single second. And . . . what I mean by that is . . . it's all right to have short . . . pauses in what you say . . . without always feeling like you have to . . . fill them up with little words like 'um.' Does that answer your question?"

"Um, yes. Thanks."

And that's when Alton *should* have stood up, said thanks again, and hurried out of that office.

But he didn't.

He said, "Except . . . um, I noticed that you say 'um' . . . *more* on some days than others. You say it most on Thursdays, usually about seven times during the announcements. On a Thursday morning."

Mrs. Buckley pressed her lips together, and she leaned farther forward, her eyes wide with disbelief. "You've been *counting* how many times I say that word—is that what you're telling me? Have you been keeping some kind of a list, or making a graph or something?"

"Um . . . well, yes."

Now it was Alton's face that got red. And he noticed that Mrs. Buckley didn't say "um" once as she shot that question at him. He also became aware that Quint was sitting so still in his chair that he could have been a statue—a statue of a very frightened boy.

Looking into Mrs. Buckley's eyes, Alton felt a wave of pure terror trying to sweep him under. But he fought the fear, and for the second time in less than two minutes, an idea burst into his mind. And this one was perfectly clear—four simple words: *Tell her the truth!*

And immediately Alton heard himself saying, "Except, I put all the data I gathered onto a kind of map. Because that's my favorite way of presenting information. And, um . . . I think I'd better warn you that this map, the one that shows how many times you say 'um' on different days during the announcements? It's . . . it's missing, and somebody might spread it around the school somehow. And . . . um, I want to say I'm sorry, just in case that happens. Really sorry. Just in case."

As Mrs. Buckley stared at him, the glass-walled

office seemed to slide into a pocket of total stillness, like the eye of a killer hurricane. Alton wasn't sure if his heart was beating. He knew he wasn't breathing—and neither was Quint.

Suddenly, Mrs. Buckley smiled. Then she started laughing, and between the snorts and chortles, she said, "A *map*? Of how many times I say 'um'? That is wonderfully silly—it's *hilarious*!" She wiped her eyes and stood up, and with a wide smile, she said, "Don't worry about your map getting spread around, Alton. Every single person in this school already knows I say 'um' too much! But if you find that map? I'd really like to see it. Now, you both need to get to homeroom, and—*um*—I've got to go meet the kindergarten bus!"

The principal was still chuckling as she grabbed her hat and gloves and hurried out.

The boys left the office. Neither of them said a word until they were halfway down the sixth-grade hall.

Then Quint said, "Dude, seriously—that was *genius*! You know that, right? *Genius*, like . . . *totally*! She could have been so mad, and instead you got her laughing! Like, if she'd been eating yogurt, it would have shot right out her nose! *That* was a miracle!"

Alton nodded and grinned. "Yeah," he said. "A miracle."

But that wasn't what Alton was thinking.

Because during that moment of pure terror in the principal's office, when he'd suddenly seen what he should say to Mrs. Buckley? He had caught a glimpse of something else, too.

And now he was certain of it.

What had just happened with Mrs. Buckley was *not* some kind of miracle. It was something else.

CHAPTER THIRTEEN

SORRY IN ADVANCE

Y ou did *what*?" Emma Wilson glared down
at Alton like he was a stinkbug.

He wanted to look friendly. And
harmless. But he tried not to smile, because that
might seem disrespectful. And he was worried that
all this thinking about controlling his face was
making him look like a robot, or maybe some
dopey character from an animated movie.

But Alton pushed all that out of his head, took
a deep breath, and then repeated himself as sin-
cerely as possible.

"I said, I put your name on a map that I made
about the heights of the kids in sixth grade.
And . . . I called you Mount Wilson. Because
the map is like one of those trail guides with
contour lines for different elevations. And since
you're the tallest kid, I used your name to mark

the high point. And I was never going to show this map to anybody, because it was more like an experiment. Except now the map is missing, and somebody might spread it around the school. So I wanted to warn you about that, and say that I'm sorry . . . in advance. In case that happens."

Still glaring, Emma snapped, "As if I *care*! Do you think you're the first stupid boy who's made fun of how tall I am?"

"Oh, it wasn't like that," said Alton quickly. "I . . . I wasn't making fun of you, honest. I think it'd be great to be as tall as you are. It's just . . . It's a fact, that's all. And I used that fact on my map, and I wanted to tell you about it. And tell you that I *wasn't* making fun of you . . . not on purpose."

"Oh, *right*," she sneered. "So you thought somebody would see 'Mount Wilson' on your map and think it *wasn't* funny at all, is that it?"

"Well . . . okay," Alton said slowly. "I *did* want it to be sort of funny. . . . And it *is* sort of funny, don't you think? I mean . . . if somebody made a picture of me? And put a globe on my shoulders instead of my head? I could smile about that—I mean, I think I could. Because it's kind of funny. Alton Ziegler *is* a total globe-head, and everybody knows it."

The thunderclouds surrounding Mount Wilson suddenly gave way to a glimmer of sunshine. But Emma's tiny smile vanished just as fast.

"I've got to go to my bus. Thanks for the warning about Mount Wilson. . . . I guess you're not a total creep after all."

The dance some guys do in the end zone after a touchdown? That's how Alton felt when Emma said he wasn't a total creep.

The talk with Emma was Alton's fifth apology of the day, and her microscopic smile was one of the better moments. The *best* moment had been during the day's first apology—Mrs. Buckley's laughing fit before school.

And as he and Quint had walked to homeroom from her office, Alton had realized that the principal's reaction hadn't been a miracle. Mrs. Buckley had forgiven him because he'd told her the truth. And he had done it in three simple steps: he'd explained about the map he'd made; he'd warned her that the map might become public; and then he'd told her he was sorry if this was going to cause her any embarrassment—*truly* sorry—in advance.

But the big breakthrough had come when Alton saw that if this process had worked with Mrs.

Buckley, then it *ought* to work just as well with everybody else. And if he could pre-apologize to all those others, too, then his missing maps would no longer have any power over him. And the blackmail would end—instantly.

He looked down again at the front of the plain gray T-shirt he was wearing. If the next fifteen minutes went well, tomorrow he could wear his favorite, the one with a map of O'Hare Airport. Because he was close to the finish line—only one more apology to go.

He'd made a list during homeroom of everybody who might get mad if his maps were released. This first list was long—so long that he thought maybe he should ask Mrs. Buckley if he could borrow the PA system and pre-apologize to the whole school at once.

Then he wondered if he really needed to apologize to *every* kid whose parents were divorced—he hadn't used anyone's name on that map. And the map about which tests got cheated on most? Same deal—there were no names. The maps about favorite shoe brands or what shirt colors were most popular? Some kids might think it was weird that he'd been studying their clothes, but would anybody feel personally offended or mad at him? Probably not.

He even decided that if his popularity map of sixth-grade lunch went public, he could deal with the reactions. Some kids might think his opinions about their popularity rankings weren't accurate, and some were sure to think the words he used for the Venn diagram circles weren't so nice, but still, most of the information wasn't really personal.

All this thinking resulted in a shorter list of possibly hurtful maps—the ones that named names—directly or indirectly. If he could pre-apologize to those people, Alton decided he could live with whatever else might happen if *all* the maps went public.

Tall Emma Wilson had needed an apology—same with short Cal of Virden Valley.

Talking with Cal had been a breeze—a simple conversation in the hall after art class.

"'Virden Valley?' Really?" Cal had scrunched up his face for a second or two, and then shrugged. "You know what? I'd rather be noticed for being short than not be noticed at all. So don't worry about it, Ziegler. Just make sure you spelled my name right."

Some of the other apologies had been harder.

After lunch he had gone into the school kitchen, and he'd told the three women who prepared lunch about his map that tracked how many trips to the bathroom sixth graders made during gym class—the period that came right after lunch every day. Alton explained that he'd noticed how certain lunch menus had the effect of causing more bathroom trips than others. And that the big winner was the chicken ravioli plate.

The lunch ladies had stood there, arms folded, listening as he tried to explain the map to them. The title of the map was "Bathroom Migration Patterns," and he had based it on this map he had about how some kinds of whales swim long distances every year looking for food. Except *his* map was about how sixth graders traveled around looking for a bathroom after eating chicken ravioli or twin tacos or American chop suey. Then he explained how the map was now missing, and that everybody in the school might end up seeing it.

After his awkward apology, and after he'd said that his map certainly was *not* meant to make fun of the good food they cooked every day for all the kids at Harper School . . . no one smiled. Alton had been planning to tell them that the school kitchen was also featured a number of times on his map of twenty-nine different smells around the building. But one woman looked like she was about to

pull off her hairnet and try to strangle him with it, so he'd said sorry one last time and made a quick exit. And walking away, Alton decided that he'd better bring his lunches from home for a while.

Thinking about that smells map, he'd almost put Elena on his apology list—he had portrayed her very perfumey self as a giant smelly flower on his map. But since she was obviously in on sending him the blackmail notes, he decided she didn't deserve an apology.

Compared to the lunch ladies, Mr. Troy had been downright friendly. When Alton talked to him after seventh-period social studies, the teacher stopped him before he'd said two sentences.

"Hold it, hold it—you made a *study* of all the clothes I wear to school? That's a little hard to believe!"

Alton said, "Well, as far as I can tell, you wear four different pairs of pants, one black belt and one brown belt, two different sport coats, eight different neckties, one pale blue shirt, one pale blue shirt with red stripes, one dark blue shirt, one plain white shirt, one white shirt with yellow stripes, and two different pairs of shoes—black loafers and brown lace-ups. Your socks are always either black or brown, depending on which shoes you wear. Except you also have one pair of yellow-and-gray argyle socks. And that's about it."

Mr. Troy scratched his chin. "Hmm . . . that's a good summary. But . . . *why*?"

Alton said, "You know how you give all those pop quizzes? I noticed that on days when there was a quiz, you were always wearing a tie."

"I see. . . . So you started keeping track?"

Alton nodded. "Yes. Since September fourteenth, 'no tie' has meant 'no quiz' ninety-five percent of the time. And you've *never* given us a quiz on a day when you're wearing the yellow-and-gray argyle socks."

Mr. Troy was smiling now. "That's pretty amazing research! But . . . why are you telling me this? Now your quiz warning system is ruined."

Alton said, "Well, I made a map called 'Stripy with a Chance of Quizzes'—because most of your ties have stripes on them. And it's laid out like a weather map of your classroom, with high- and low-pressure areas. And the chance of a quiz is drawn like a cold front—with neckties along the line instead of those little pointy arrows they use on real weather maps. And your yellow-and-gray argyle socks are also on the line. I've never shown the map to anybody, but somebody stole it the

other day, and I think they might put it up in the school somewhere. And I wanted to apologize in advance, in case that happens. For kind of making fun of your clothes."

"Apologize?" Mr. Troy grinned. "I should thank you—I didn't know I was such a creature of habit!"

That had been apology number four, and then Emma had been number five.

And now he had only one more: Miss Wheeling. It was the hardest one—which is why Alton had put it off until the end of the day.

Showing the topics that filled up somebody's brain? That was a lot more personal than talking about someone's clothes or how tall they were or even how much they said "um."

And the drawing of her frizzy hairdo? Also very personal. And then listing all those things that she had never mentioned in class? That was way over the line—not just personal, but also kind of mean. And then showing that map to Quint? Thinking about it made him feel awful. Alton was pretty sure he was about to get yelled at—and he was completely sure he deserved it.

And, as if explaining about the brain map wasn't bad enough, he was *also* going to have to tell her all about the fire drill, about why he'd missed it on purpose. And why he had then lied to her by pretending he'd been so involved in making a new map.

He stood in the hall outside her room, trying to find the courage to walk in. He was reaching for the doorknob, when he heard someone call to him.

"Yo—Al!"

He didn't need to look to know it was Quint. Alton turned, and even though the hall was still crowded with kids headed for the buses, he spotted Quint frantically waving from down near the gym.

He called again. "Yo—come quick!"

Glad to delay his last big apology, Alton hurried toward him, and when he got there, Quint grabbed his arm and pulled him around the corner.

"What's the mat—"

"Just listen, okay?" Quint was out of breath, and he talked quickly. "I went to the library to turn in some books, and when I was leaving, Mrs. Lomax said, 'Do you know if Alton got his folder back?'"

"What?!" Alton stared at him. *"She had th—"*

"Shh—just listen!" Quint said. "So, I played dumb, and Mrs. Lomax said, 'Alton left a folder

here Monday, when you two were making so much noise.' And I said, 'Want me to take it to him?' And you know what she said?"

"What, *what*?"

"She said, 'Alton didn't come for it, so I gave it to Miss Wheeling.' And I said, 'On Monday?' and she said, 'No, Tuesday after school'!" Quint paused dramatically. "Get it? Miss Wheeling got your folder *Tuesday* after school! And when did you get the first ransom note? *Wednesday morning!* She's the one, dude—*she's the mapnapper!*"

CHAPTER FOURTEEN

FROM HERE

N*o way!*"

Quint said it again. "She's got the maps—it's Miss Wheeling!"

Alton felt dizzy, weak. He slumped against the wall next to the gym.

"Are you okay?" Quint asked. "I should get to my bus—but I can miss it."

Alton pulled himself upright and shook his head. "No, you go ahead. I'm good."

"You sure?"

Alton managed a smile. "I'm fine—it's just . . . crazy, that's all."

"Yeah—*and* insane and nutso and bonkers—*totally!*"

Alton's mood caught hold of him.

Then in a hushed tone Quint said, "So . . . what're you going to do?"

"Not sure," said Alton.

"You should go home and think—that's my advice. Look, I've gotta boogie. Call me, okay? And whatever you do, think first."

Alton nodded. "I will—thanks."

Once Quint was around the corner, Alton leaned against the wall again. It helped stop the spinning. He closed his eyes, but that made the spinning worse, so he opened them and stared down at a place where four floor tiles came together.

Instantly, he thought of the Four Corners, the place where the corners of Utah, Colorado, New Mexico, and Arizona meet. He had stood at that exact spot two summers ago when his family had gone to the Grand Canyon—a great moment for a kid who loved maps.

Outside, the last of the buses rumbled away. Inside, the hallways went from noisy to almost silent in less than two minutes, and Alton spent that time staring at those four lines on the floor, wishing he had never laid eyes on a map.

"You have a problem here?"

Alton stood up straight and spun to his left.

The gym teacher squinted at his face. "You don't look so good, Ziegler. Need help?"

"I'm okay, Mr. Ludlow. Thanks."

"You miss your bus?"

"Um . . . I had to stay after school . . . to talk to Miss Wheeling."

"Then you'd better get moving." He pointed. "Thataway."

"Right," said Alton. "See you tomorrow." And he started walking.

He turned the corner, and after about ten steps, he decided to take the next right turn toward the front hall. Because Quint was right. He needed some time to think before he could talk with Miss Wheeling. He needed to go home. So . . . he could call his mom . . . except, she wouldn't want to come until after Beth got off the bus at home.

So it made just as much sense to wait for the late bus—forty-five minutes. . . . That wasn't so long.

I'll just wait in the office.

At the place where the hallways met, Alton started to turn right, but then he stopped and glanced in each direction. The halls were empty.

Again, he thought of the Four Corners . . . and the four points on a compass.

A feeling came over him, so strong and clear, and he stood still and looked down at his feet. He felt like he was standing on an enormous map—

sort of the way he'd felt as he'd ridden his bike over to Quint's house on Tuesday. But this time, it was a map of his entire life, like a complete GPS track of where he'd been so far—every single step he had ever taken. All those hundreds of thousands of steps had brought him to this exact place in time and space, this one spot. *And I'm the only one who can figure out the right way to go from here.*

Alton turned and kept walking—but not toward the office. He headed for Miss Wheeling's room. It was time to make his last apology of the day.

CHAPTER FIFTEEN

CONFESSIONS

H i, Miss Wheeling—can I talk to you about something?"

She looked up and smiled, then looked at the clock. "Sure, come on in. But I've got to leave in about five minutes. My dog-sitter has a dentist appointment—for herself, not the dog!"

She laughed, but Alton barely smiled.

Knowing that she had his maps and that she'd sent those notes to him? It changed the way she looked to him. And it did *not* make him feel like laughing.

He just couldn't believe a *teacher* would do something like that. It was . . . impossible. Now, some girl like Elena? Yes, he could believe that. But a girl like . . .

Sliding into a desk in the front row, Alton gulped and looked at Miss Wheeling—really *looked* at her. Because that thought he'd had a second ago? He had almost said . . . *a* girl *like Miss Wheeling*!

Sitting there six feet away behind that big boxy desk, Miss Wheeling really did look much more like a girl than a teacher—or at least most of the other teachers Alton had ever known. Because none of those other women teachers had been so young—a lot of them were married with kids of their own, and some of them had been almost ready to retire.

Alton realized he was staring at Miss Wheeling and that he couldn't sit there for ten minutes and try to figure everything out. He had to say something—and no matter what *she* had done, *he* still had plenty to apologize for. So he jumped right in.

"I came to say I'm sorry. Because about three weeks ago I made a map, sort of a cartoony-type map. And it was about things you'd said in class."

Miss Wheeling's eyebrows shot up. "Really? You mean math and science?"

He shook his head, amazed at how she could keep pretending that she had no idea what he was talking about. "No . . . you see, back in September I started keeping a list of everything you said that *wasn't* about our schoolwork."

Her eyebrows lifted even higher. "*Everything? Like what?*"

Alton said, "Things like your dog and your little brother. And food and football—stuff like that. And using that information, I made . . . a map of your brain."

"A *what?*"

Alton flinched at her tone, but he wasn't afraid because he knew she was just acting.

"A map of your brain. Divided up into the seven things you think about the most . . . based on what I heard you talk about in class."

Her lips pressed into a straight, sharp line. "I want to see this map right *now!*"

Alton had to look away—he didn't want to show his feelings by the expression in his eyes. Because he knew she'd *seen* that map—it was probably in her desk drawer, right there in front of her!

He managed to glance at her, and kept talking. "That's the thing, Miss Wheeling. The map is . . . missing. And the person who has it might try to spread it around the school." He gulped and then said, "And the map I made of your brain? It's even worse, because I drew a picture of your hair, too. Sort of surrounding the brain . . . on the map."

Miss Wheeling's face got red, but before she could speak, Alton rushed ahead—he wanted to get his part over all at once, like pulling a loose tooth, just like he would have if this were a *real* apology about a map she'd never seen.

"And . . . on the map there's also a list of things you *never* talk about—like movies you saw, or books or a hobby or . . . a boyfriend. And the fire drill on Tuesday? I lied about that. I stayed inside the school on purpose so I could search for that map—and for a bunch of other maps too. I was never going to show them to anyone . . . except, I showed your brain map to Quint Harrison on Monday, and after that . . . they all got *stolen*."

He let that last word hang in the air, and he watched her face. She didn't flinch, didn't blink, didn't twitch a muscle. Amazing!

So he went on. "And I hope no one spreads any of them around, especially the map about your brain. Because I never meant it to be public. And it's all my fault for showing it to Quint. And I'm sorry. Really sorry. About everything."

As he said that last part, Alton meant every word. Even though she'd been paying him back with the notes and all the worrying he'd done over the past two days, this whole mess began with him. It really was his fault, and he felt bad about that.

Miss Wheeling opened the top drawer of her desk, and he thought, *Here we go—now it's her confession time!*

But she took out her phone and stabbed at the little screen.

Alton panicked.

Is she calling the principal? Is she going to turn this whole thing around—maybe accuse me of complete disrespect for a teacher? And maybe try to get me expelled or something? Is she that angry about that map?

"Charlotte? Hi. You can go ahead and leave now. I'm still here at school, so just put Mr. Wiggles in his crate before you go, okay? Good . . . That's great. . . . Thanks."

Slowly, she put her phone back into the drawer. And sitting very still, she looked down at her folded hands.

Alton had no clue what she was going to say or do next.

He said, "Miss Wheeling, I'm really—"

She raised one hand, like a traffic cop, then brought it down slowly.

Then she looked at him for a few moments, and again, Alton couldn't tell what she was thinking.

But when she spoke, her voice was even and calm.

"First of all, thank you for telling me the truth about the fire drill. A little while after you came in to apologize after school on Tuesday, I realized you hadn't been completely honest about that. I lost the key to my classroom about three weeks ago, and it was the second time in less than a month, and I haven't been able to tell the janitor yet. So I've been leaving my classroom unlocked during the day. And after the fire drill, I found my door locked, so *you* must have locked it. . . . And therefore, you had *not* been lost in your own mind, drawing some new map all that time. I suspected you'd been up to something. So thank you for the explanation."

There was another long pause.

Now the signals weren't good. Alton saw her bite her lower lip, then her jaw muscles got tense. She reached one hand up and touched her hair—which was incredibly frizzy today.

Then she looked him in the eyes and smiled a little. "And about this brain map you made? Thanks for telling me about that, too. It was brave of you. It's no secret that this is my first year as a teacher, and I'm probably still too sensitive about what others think of me. That little brother

I mention so much? He still teases me all the time, especially about my hair—he calls me Fathead! And I don't like teasing. But I hope I'll get better about ignoring it—I think I'll have to!"

Abruptly, she took her phone out of the drawer again and stood up. "So, I accept your apology. I've got to leave now. . . . Is there anything else?"

Alton was stunned—she wasn't even going to mention the folder!

"Um . . . I . . . no . . . I guess that's everything."

He got up too, and as he did, Miss Wheeling stepped around her desk, stood in front of him, and held out her hand. Instinctively, he looked her in the eyes, took her hand, and gave her a strong, firm handshake, just like his dad had taught him to.

She smiled and said, "Again, thank you, Alton."

But their handshake felt phony to him, and her smile seemed forced. It was more like *half* a thank-you.

He smiled back at her anyway and stammered, "Y-you're welcome."

She let go of his hand, walked quickly to the back of the room, and opened the closet where she kept her coat.

Alton picked up his backpack and headed for

the door. He felt totally confused, but he did remember that he hadn't gotten his jacket after eighth period. He went to his cubby, pulled it off the coat hook—and stared.

The folder.

Only an edge was sticking out from under some books and papers, but he recognized it instantly. Glancing over his shoulder, he saw Miss Wheeling looking through her purse. He pulled the folder out and stuck it into his backpack.

As he hurried toward the door, Miss Wheeling looked up and smiled. "See you tomorrow, Alton."

He nodded awkwardly. "See you tomorrow."

Alton texted to let his mom know he'd had to stay at school, and then he waited in the office for the late bus—which gave him a good long while to think. The bus finally arrived, and fifteen minutes into the ride home, his phone buzzed—a text from Quint.

YO DUDE—WHAT'S UP?

DID U GO HOME?

NO. TALKED WITH MISS W.

WHAAAT?
DID SHE GIVE IT UP?

                                        NO.

WHAAAT?!!

                        SHE SAID NOTHING.

SO THEN U JAMMED HER ABOUT EVERYTHING,
RIGHT?

                                        NO.

WHAAAT???

                    I APOLOGIZED, SHE ACCEPTED.
            THEN I FOUND THE FOLDER IN MY CUBBY.
                MAYBE IT WAS THERE SINCE TUESDAY.
                MAYBE SHE NEVER EVEN LOOKED IN IT.

EXCEPT U KNOW SHE HAD IT!
CUZ U KNOW IT WASN'T IN YR CUBBY.
AND U GOT THOSE NOTES!

                                WHAT NOTES?

WHAAAT? DA NOTES!!!

FROM EL MAPNAPPO!

              I DON'T HAVE ANY NOTES FROM HER.

                    DO YOU?

NO . . . WAIT—WHAAAT??

I'M NOT GETTIN THIS, DUDE!

                    IT'S OVER.

         IT HAS TO BE LIKE IT DIDN'T HAPPEN.

            AND I'M GOOD WITH THAT.

CLICK—GOTCHA.

SO . . . CAN I SEE THE REST OF THOSE MAPS

SOMETIME?

                MAPS? WHAT MAPS?

WHAAAT? IN YR FOLDER!

                  WHAT FOLDER?

OH—RIGHT. IT DIDN'T HAPPEN.

LATER, DUDE.

                  LATER—DUDE.

CHAPTER SIXTEEN

THE REST OF THE WAY

November to June is a long time, but it didn't feel that way to Alton. The rest of sixth grade went flashing past.

Quint Harrison turned out to be a real friend, the best one Alton had ever had. By the end of the year, Alton was using a lot more slang, and Quint was using a lot less.

The abandoned-railroads project ended up being a pretty big deal. The main part, of course, was a map, and the design Quint and Alton came up with did a great job of blending present-day hiking and biking information with the history of the old railroad companies. The map also showed how the railroads had changed the state's economy and politics and how life had been improved for generations of farmers, miners, meat-packers, and factory workers. Mr. Troy thought the map was so good that he sent a copy to the Illinois Department of Natural Resources. Three weeks later the department director herself sent a letter to Alton and Quint asking for permission to post a version of their map online for the public to enjoy—with both of their names on it. They said yes.

Mrs. Buckley stopped Alton in the hall one day near the end of January.

"You know, Alton, you never brought me that map about how much I said 'um'—did you forget?"

Alton smiled and shook his head. "No, I remembered. But I think that map might never be seen again." Which was true—mostly.

He had taken his folder of secret maps straight home that afternoon in October, but he couldn't make himself rip them up. Instead he'd hidden them deep inside a box of his old second- and third-grade school projects that his mom had tucked away in the attic. He imagined that in five or ten years, they might be interesting to look at again. Just not anytime soon. And they would be seen by no one but him.

Before the principal walked away, Alton remembered something important. He said, "Um . . . there's something else I need to tell you about that map. Remember the first fire drill back in October? I think Miss Wheeling got in trouble because I didn't go outside with the rest of her class that day. Well . . . I stayed inside on purpose during the drill so I could hunt for that map, and bunch of other ones too. So it wasn't Miss Wheeling's fault. And I wanted you to know that."

Mrs. Buckley frowned. "You should have told me about this sooner. Did you explain this to Miss Wheeling?"

Alton nodded. "Yes, a couple days after it happened."

"Really?" Mrs. Buckley looked puzzled. "Because she never mentioned it to me." Then the principal smiled. "Maybe that's because Miss Wheeling didn't want to get *you* in trouble. Well, I'm very glad to know about this, Alton—thank you. And I'll get it all sorted out."

March brought the annual crush of standardized testing, and after that, it felt like the days flipped by faster and faster.

Sometime in April, Alton decided that Elena was sort of cute, and he mentioned it to Quint one day.

He narrowed his eyes and looked at Alton. "So, talk to her."

"But, like . . . what would I say?"

Quint thought a second. "I got it! Tell her that once upon a time *she* was on this map you made!"

The next day Alton did just that, and the two of them had a long conversation with a lot of laughing. Alton even got brave enough to tell Elena she'd been featured on that map because her perfume had seemed kind of strong to him.

On a Saturday afternoon in May he and Quint met up at the mall with Elena and Catherine to get pizza, and Alton noticed that Elena wasn't wearing any perfume at all. He decided he kind of missed it. And he told her so.

Alton had stopped keeping a record of the things Miss Wheeling talked about. He even stopped thinking about her hair—and it looked like she had, too. She wore it the same way every day, pulled back into a tight little ponytail that was held in place with an industrial-strength rubber band.

Except Alton couldn't help noticing that Miss Wheeling still went on and on and on about how great the metric system was, and how Americans needed to wake up and measure everything the way the rest of the world did. Alton decided she was right, and to do his part, every new map he made included both English and metric measurements.

And Alton Robert Ziegler did make new maps—plenty of them. While the ground was still frozen, he charted all the wetlands areas in and around Harper's Grove, and when the weather warmed up, he used a sound-level meter app on his smartphone to rate how loud the spring frogs sang at each location.

In April he rode his bike up and down every single street in town, recording his cell phone's signal strength each half-block, and then organized all the information on a color-coded grid.

And late one night he printed out all fifty-seven names and addresses from the contacts list in his phone, and located each of them on a map of the United States.

Then he realized that he was paying *way* too much attention to his phone.

And speaking of his phone, one day in late May he got a text from Heather. She said she had just scored a FTF—a "First to Find," which is a big deal in the world of geocaching. She had spotted a mysterious geocache posting on an obscure website—a geocache that had been hidden by none other than SirMapsAlot. It had taken her a while to figure it all out, but the clues and the coordinates had led Heather to Mrs. Buckley's office and to a chair just left of her desk. And Alton had grinned and texted back, CONGRATS! Because he remembered very clearly how he had stuck one of those little magnetic key boxes onto the bottom of that chair the day he and Quint had visited Mrs. Buckley. And inside the box he'd left a log—a folded yellow note card with the office coordinates written on it—along with some swag: three of his customized rubber bands.

Heather had texted again: SO HOW DID YOU GET THAT HIDDEN IN THE PRINCIPAL'S OFFICE??

And Alton had replied: IT'S A LONG STORY—ASK ME AGAIN IN FIVE YEARS!

For a while during the spring, Alton got stuck on the idea of using circles instead of rectangles as the main shape for his maps. One of his circle maps was the sixth-grade lunch period shown as a set of ten different-size circles, each with the same center, and the size of each ring indicated the noise level in the cafeteria at three-minute intervals. And how did he measure the sound intensity? With his phone, of course.

But mostly, Alton stayed away from making maps about school. There was a very large world out there, and it began demanding nearly all his attention.

Suddenly, it was June, and then it was the last half day of school.

Miss Wheeling and Mr. Troy had a party in the library for the graduating sixth graders. Standing around, eating doughnuts and drinking juice with Quint and Elena, Alton felt great about everything. It had been a terrific school year—the best one yet.

But all during the party, Alton kept hoping Miss Wheeling would quietly pull him aside and whisper, *You already know this, Alton, but* I *was the one who sent you those notes, who made you stop wearing your map T-shirts for two days, and who sent you to ask Mrs. Buckley about her "um"-ing! And I'm sorry about that, and I really do forigve you with all my heart—for everything!*

But it never happened. The party ended, and everyone went to back to their homerooms to do a final cleanout of the cubbies and to get their report cards.

Alton had heard that in the neighboring town of Wayview, the schools had stopped sending report cards home with kids—the parents were e-mailed or texted a code, and then they accessed their kids' grade reports online. And sitting there, he thought that it would make an interesting map—to see which towns in the state had shifted to e-grades. . . .

He still liked the old system.

As Miss Wheeling handed him his sealed envelope, there was no special smile, no little wink, nothing to indicate that anything out of the ordinary had passed between them way back during that last week of October.

But *something* had . . . right?

The way it worked in his family, report cards didn't get opened up until both his mom and dad were home. Alton was in no hurry, and he certainly wasn't worried. He knew he'd been doing good work, and he was sure he had gotten good grades—in fact, mostly As.

And around five thirty, that was what he and his mom and dad saw.

"This is great, Alton," said his mom. "We're very proud of you!"

His little sister's grades were excellent too— one check, and all the rest check-plusses.

His dad grinned at both of them. "This calls for pizza and ice cream and a movie—all in favor, shout aye!"

"*Aye!*"

"Great! Everybody in the car in exactly four minutes . . . from—*now*!"

"Wait a second. . . ." His mom frowned.

She was squinting at Alton's report card, and she held it out to him, pointing.

"What in the world does *this* mean?"

On the back of the report card he saw a sketch, roughly drawn with pencil, but definitely the image of a brain—*his* brain! It had been divided up into five sections, from largest to smallest: MAPS, PIZZA, CELL PHONE, GIRLS, and near the bottom, a tiny little area labeled SCIENCE CLASS.

He grinned. "That's just Miss Wheeling's idea of a joke—it doesn't mean anything."

That was what Alton said, but it simply wasn't true.

Nothing could have meant more.

Reading Group Guide
for
The Map Trap

Discussion Topics

1. Chapter 2 has the following quote:

> **"He discovered that making a good map was complicated, much more complicated than he had ever imagined. And even though he didn't like math very much, he made himself learn about fractions and measurement so that his maps could be as accurate as possible. He didn't really notice it, but during fourth grade, maps began to turn him into a very precise thinker and a very careful observer."**

What does this tell us about Alton? Why does map-making require precision, observation, and math? Do all maps require this? What skills does it take to read a map? Is it the same as reading a story?

2. The title of Chapter Three is "Like Switzerland." What does this mean? What word in the chapter helps our understanding of this chapter title, and what do the characters do to further our understanding of the way things look versus the way things are?

3. Discuss Alton, the main character in the story, and how his actions contribute to the sequence of events.

4. In Chapter 13, Alton decides to "pre-apologize." What do you think this means? Why do you think Alton feels it's necessary to do this? Is pre-apologizing a good strategy?

5. How do Alton and Quint respond to the events and challenges of the missing maps and the ransom notes? Are their ideas right? What would you do if something of yours was taken and you started to receive ransom notes? Why didn't they report the theft to the teacher? Who else could they have asked for help?

6. Alton not only diagrammed the students in the lunchroom with a Venn diagram, but he was

precise with his language and descriptions. How would you feel if you were in a map that you felt didn't really represent you? What would you do, and how would you change things?

7. Technology has evolved so much that it's part of our everyday lives. We have access to maps and directions on cell phones, laptops, tablets, GPS devices, and computers. Discuss how maps and GPS have impacted your life. Think about the ways that you have used these maps and devices in your home or school life, and how you've benefited from this technology. Is this form of progress good or bad? How are your experiences the same or different from that of Alton in *The Map Trap*?

Turn the page for a look at
another Andrew Clements novel

ABOUT AVERAGE

It was a sunny spring morning, but there was murder in the air. Jordan Johnston was killing *Pomp and Circumstance*. Actually, the whole elementary school orchestra was involved. It was a musical massacre.

But Jordan's violin was especially deadly. It screeched like a frightened owl. Mr. Graisha glared at her, snapping his baton up and down, side to side, fighting to keep all twenty-three students playing in unison. It was a losing battle. He glanced up at the clock and then waved both arms as if he needed to stop a freight train.

"All right, all right, stop playing—everyone, stop. *Stop!*" He mopped his forehead with a handkerchief and smiled as best he could. "I think that's enough for this morning. Don't forget that this is Thursday, and we have a special rehearsal right

here after school—*don't* be late. And if you have any free time at all during the day, please *practice*. We are *not* going to play well *together* if you can't play well *by yourself*, right? Practice!"

Jordan put away her violin carefully. She loved the instrument, and she was very good at putting it away. She was also good at polishing the rich brown wood and keeping the strings in tune, and keeping the bow in tip-top condition. It was playing the thing that gave her trouble.

But she was *not* going to give up on it.

She had given up on so many things during the past eight months. The violin was her last stand, her line in the sand. She was bound and determined to become a gifted violinist—instead of a scary one.

She was still a member of the sixth-grade chorus, but she didn't feel that was much of an accomplishment. Every other sixth grader was in it too.

Jordan wasn't shy about singing. She sang right out. She sang so loudly that Mr. Graisha had taken her aside one day. He was in charge of all things musical at Baird Elementary School—band, orchestra, chorus, everything.

"Jordan, you have great . . . enthusiasm. But it would be good if you didn't sing louder than all the other kids around you. The audience needs to hear them too, don't you think?"

Jordan got the message: *Your* voice isn't so good.

She almost always sang the correct notes, she was sure of that. She wasn't a terrible singer—just not good enough to be the loudest one. Her voice was about average.

Her friend Kylie had a gorgeous voice, high and sweet and clear—but she was so timid. Kylie barely made a squeak during chorus practice, and she hardly whispered at concerts. It drove Jordan crazy.

She wanted to grab her by the shoulders and shake her and shout, "Kylie, if *I* had a voice like yours, I would already live in Hollywood—no kidding, I would be a *star* by now! What is *wrong* with you?"

Jordan was a careful observer of all the talented kids at her school—the ones who got the trophies and awards, the ones who were written up in the local newspaper, the ones who were obviously going to go on and do amazing and wonderful things all the rest of their lives. *They* were the gifted ones, the talented ones, the special ones.

And she was not one of them.

After her violin was tucked safely into its bulletproof case, Jordan began putting away the music stands. She carried them one by one and stacked them over in the dark corner of the stage next to the heavy folds of the red velvet curtain. When all twenty-three stands were arranged neatly, she folded the metal chairs and then stacked each one onto a rolling cart. She also tipped Mr. Graisha's heavy podium up onto its rollers and wheeled it over to its place next to the grand piano.

It was already warm in the auditorium, and she leaned against the piano a moment. Moving that wooden podium always made her feel like a weight lifter, and she didn't want to start sweating so early in the day. It had been hotter than normal all week long.

Jordan had volunteered at the start of the school year to be the orchestra stage manager. She arrived early for each rehearsal and set up the chairs and the music stands. Then, after rehearsal, she stayed to put them all away again.

She didn't do this to get on Mr. Graisha's good side—the only sure way to do *that* was to be a super-talented musician. She just liked helping out. She also liked the stage to be orderly. She knew how to arrange the chairs and music stands correctly, and she understood how to put everything away again, just right.

Her best friend, Nikki Scanlon, had wanted to be the co-manager, but Jordan enjoyed doing the work herself. Also, by the time she finished putting things away three mornings a week, Jordan was sometimes by herself, alone on the big stage. She enjoyed that, too.

And today, like the other times she'd been alone in there, she went to the center of the stage and looked out over all the empty seats.

Baird Elementary School had once been the town's high school, and the auditorium was in a separate building off to one side. It was a large room. Row after row of theater seats sloped up to the back wall.

Jordan smiled modestly and walked to the front edge of the stage. Looking out over the crowd, she lowered her eyes then took a long, graceful bow.

The people were standing up now, whistling and hooting and clapping like crazy. She smiled and bowed again, then gave a special nod to her mom and dad, there in the front row. She even smiled sweetly at her big sister, Allie, and her little brother, Tim. Of course, Tim didn't notice. He

was only four, and he was staring at the blue-and-red stage lights with one finger stuck in his nose.

A young girl in a blue dress ran down the center aisle from the back of the hall, stretched up on tiptoes, and handed Jordan two dozen yellow roses—her favorite flower. With the bouquet cradled in one arm, Jordan took a final bow and backed away. The red velvet curtain parted for just a moment, and she slipped backstage.

There were people asking for autographs, plus some journalists with their cameras flashing, and a crush of happy friends, eager to congratulate her and wish her well. It was wonderful, and Jordan savored each second, as she had so many times before.

Brrnnnnng!

The first bell—six seconds of harsh, brain-rattling noise. It echoed in the empty auditorium. Outside behind the main building, kids whooped and yelled as they ran from the playground and lined up at the doors.

The intruding sounds did not touch Jordan's joy and certainty. She felt absolutely sure that one day her moment of triumph would be real, a part of her life.

But why would all those people be applauding *her*? She had no idea.

J ordan's memory was a powerful force. A moment from the past would sneak up and kidnap her and then force her to think about it until she discovered something she didn't know she knew.

On this particular June morning, a thought grabbed her as she pushed open the heavy stage door and began walking to the main school building. She remembered a book she had read near the end of fifth grade.

It was a famous one, *Sarah, Plain and Tall*, and for a couple of days there, Jordan had wished her mom was dead. Not really. But that's what had happened in that story, and it caught her imagination.

This dad lived with his daughter and son, and they all felt sad because the mom had died. But there was a woman, Sarah, coming to visit, and she *might* become the dad's new wife—a new mom.

It was deliciously sad. Jordan loved sad stories.

Jordan also loved this woman in the book right away, this Sarah. She was plain, and she knew it, and she didn't try to hide it from anybody. She even came right out and said it to the man who might become her husband: *I'm plain. And tall.*

Jordan was plain too. That's what this memory was forcing her to think about.

But it wasn't like being plain was some new discovery for Jordan. She had always known that. She was plain, but, unlike Sarah, she wasn't tall. She wasn't short, either.

She was Jordan, Plain and Average.

Being pretty and being tall were two of the ways Jordan did not feel special, and they both felt important. Especially prettiness.

Her face was her face, and there wasn't much she could do about it.

Of course, she had seen TV shows about how women could change their faces. And sometimes a woman looked better afterward . . . sort of. Except she never looked quite like *herself* anymore.

Jordan couldn't imagine ever doing that. She had a smaller version of her dad's nose, and she knew she'd miss that if it went away. Also her mom's eyebrows. Jordan knew she wasn't going to be famous for her beauty. And she was okay with that . . . until she started thinking about boys.

There was one particular boy, Jonathan Cardley. He played cello in the orchestra. As Jordan walked toward the main school building that morning, she spotted him with his friends over near the playground doors.

Jonathan had straight brown hair. Sometimes it hung down a little too far onto his forehead and covered his eyes, which she didn't like. They were nice eyes, a greenish-blue color. He was taller than most of the other sixth-grade boys, and Jordan thought he always looked good, no matter what he was wearing. He looked especially good when he wore jeans and a white collared shirt, like today.

Jonathan seemed to care a lot about prettiness. Most of the time he only talked to the nicest-looking girls—including Kylie, her friend with the gorgeous voice.

But at least Jonathan knew who Jordan was. He even talked to her now and then. He would say, "Hey, Jordan—have you seen Kylie?"

Kylie, Cute and Tall.

Jordan wished that all the really pretty girls

would disappear, one by one, until *she* was left as the cutest girl at school. Then Jonathan Cardley would be asking some other girl, "Hey, have you seen Jordan?"

A lot of girls would have to vanish.

Jordan pulled open the heavy door at the end of the walkway, took a left, and headed for the sixth-grade hall. It was a separate part of the school because all the sixth graders switched classes this year, just like they would next year at the junior high.

Jordan wasn't looking forward to homeroom today. She never looked forward to homeroom.

Kylie would be there, same as always, but she wasn't the problem. Ever since they'd become friends during fourth grade, Kylie had never said one mean word, never teased her about a single mess-up, never made her feel plain or untalented or awkward.

Kylie, Kind and Cool.

And Kylie had been nice to her when they'd been on the sixth-grade soccer team back in September and October, and then during basketball season, too. Of course, Kylie had been a star on both teams—Kylie, Strong and Skilled.

No, the problem with homeroom wasn't Kylie. The problem was . . . *someone else.*

Jordan did not want to even *think* the name.

Because this had been a good day so far. Yes, it was too warm, but it was bright and sunny, and it was one day closer to summer vacation. And the best part of the day so far? She had managed to avoid *that person* during orchestra practice. Now, if she could just make it through homeroom without any contact, then they'd be in different classes until gym.

As Jordan went toward the sixth-grade hall, she made herself walk more slowly. She also planned to stop into the girls' room. She wanted to arrive at homeroom just as the bell rang. She did not want to spend one extra second anywhere near *her*.